Books by Eleanor H. Porter

PUBLISHED BY

HOUGHTON MIFFLIN COMPANY

MARY MARIE. Illustrated.
DAWN. Illustrated.
THE TANGLED THREADS. Illustrated.
THE TIE THAT BINDS. Illustrated.
ACROSS THE YEARS. Illustrated.
OH, MONEY! MONEY! Illustrated.
THE ROAD TO UNDERSTANDING. Illustrated.
JUST DAVID. Illustrated.

MARY MARIE

"IF I CONSULTED NO ONE'S WISHES BUT MY OWN, I SHOULD KEEP HER HERE ALWAYS" (page 143)

MARY MARIE

BY

ELEANOR H. PORTER

With Illustrations by
Helen Mason Grose

BOSTON AND NEW YORK
HOUGHTON MIFFLIN COMPANY
The Riverside Press Cambridge
1920

TO MY FRIEND
ELIZABETH S. BOWEN

CONTENTS

ILLUSTRATIONS

From drawings by HELEN MASON GROSE

MARY MARIE

. .

PREFACE

WHICH EXPLAINS THINGS

FATHER calls me Mary. Mother calls me Marie.
Everybody else calls me Mary Marie. The rest
of my name is Anderson.

I'm thirteen years old, and I'm a cross-current and a contradiction. That is, Sarah says I'm
that. (Sarah is my old nurse.) She says she read
it once — that the children of unlikes were always a cross-current and a contradiction. And
my father and mother are unlikes, and I'm the
children. That is, I'm the child. I'm all there is.
And now I'm going to be a bigger cross-current
and contradiction than ever, for I'm going to
live half the time with Mother and the other half
with Father. Mother will go to Boston to live,
and Father will stay here — a divorce, you know.

I'm terribly excited over it. None of the other
girls have got a divorce in their families, and I
always did like to be different. Besides, it ought
to be awfully interesting, more so than just living
along, common, with your father and mother in

the same house all the time — especially if it's been anything like my house with my father and mother in it!

That's why I've decided to make a book of it — that is, it really will be a book, only I shall have to call it a diary, on account of Father, you know. Won't it be funny when I don't have to do things on account of Father? And I won't, of course, the six months I'm living with Mother in Boston. But, oh, my! — the six months I'm living here with him — whew! But, then, I can stand it. I may even like it — some. Anyhow, it'll be *different*. And that's something.

Well, about making this into a book. As I started to say, he would n't let me. I know he would n't. He says novels are a silly waste of time, if not absolutely wicked. But, a diary — oh, he loves diaries! He keeps one himself, and he told me it would be an excellent and instructive discipline for me to do it, too — set down the weather and what I did every day.

The weather and what I did every day, indeed! Lovely reading that would make, would n't it? Like this:

"The sun shines this morning. I got up, ate my breakfast, went to school, came home, ate my dinner, played one hour over to Carrie Heywood's, practiced on the piano one hour, studied another hour. Talked with Mother upstairs in her room about the sunset and the snow on the trees. Ate my supper. Was talked *to* by Father down in the library about improving myself and taking care not to be light-minded and frivolous. (He meant like Mother, only he did n't say it right out loud. You don't have to say some things right out in plain words, you know.) Then I went to bed."

Just as if I was going to write my novel like that! Not much I am. But I shall call it a diary. Oh, yes, I shall call it a diary — till I take it to be printed. Then I shall give it its true name — a novel. And I'm going to tell the printer that I've left it for him to make the spelling right, and put in all those tiresome little commas and periods and quotation marks that everybody seems to make such a fuss about. If I write the story part, I can't be expected to be bothered with looking up how words are spelt, every five minutes, nor fussing over putting in a whole lot of foolish little dots and dashes.

As if anybody who was reading the story cared for that part! The story 's the thing.

I love stories. I've written lots of them for the girls, too — little short ones, I mean; not a long one like this is going to be, of course. And it'll be so exciting to be living a story instead of reading it — only when you 're *living* a story you can't peek over to the back to see how it's all coming out. I shan't like that part. Still, it may be all the more exciting, after all, *not* to know what's coming.

I like love stories the best. Father's got — oh, lots of books in the library, and I've read stacks of them, even some of the stupid old histories and biographies. I had to read them when there was n't anything else to read. But there were n't many love stories. Mother's got a few, though — lovely ones — and some books of poetry, on the little shelf in her room. But I read all those ages ago.

That's why I'm so thrilled over this new one — the one I'm living, I mean. For of course this will be a love story. There'll be *my* love story in two or three years, when I grow up, and while I'm waiting there's Father's and Mother's.

Nurse Sarah says that when you're divorced you're free, just like you were before you were married, and that sometimes they marry again. That made me think right away: what if Father or Mother, or both of them, married again? And I should be there to see it, and the courting, and all! Would n't that be some love story? Well, I just guess!

And only think how all the girls would envy me — and they just living along their humdrum, everyday existence with fathers and mothers already married and living together, and nothing exciting to look forward to. For really, you know, when you come right down to it, there *are n't* many girls that have got the chance I've got.

And so that's why I've decided to write it into a book. Oh, yes, I know I'm young — only thirteen. But I *feel* really awfully old; and you know a woman is as old as she feels. Besides, Nurse Sarah says I am old for my age, and that it's no wonder, the kind of a life I've lived.

And maybe that is so. For of course it *has* been different, living with a father and mother that are getting ready to be divorced from what it would have been living with the loving, happy-ever-after kind. Nurse Sarah says it's a shame and a pity, and that it's the children that always suffer. But I'm not suffering — not a mite. I'm just enjoying it. It's so exciting.

Of course if I was going to lose either one, it would be different. But I'm not, for I am to live with Mother six months, then with Father.

So I still have them both. And, really, when you come right down to it, I'd *rather* take them separate that way. Why, separate they're just perfectly all right, like that — that — what-do-you-call-it powder? — sedlitzer, or something like that. Anyhow, it's that white powder that you mix in two glasses, and that looks just like water till you put them together. And then, oh, my! such a fuss and fizz and splutter! Well, it's that way with Father and Mother. It'll be lots easier to take them separate, I know. For now I can be Mary six months, then Marie six months, and not try to be them both all at once, with maybe only five minutes between them.

And I think I shall love both Father and Mother better separate, too. Of course I love Mother, and I know I'd just adore Father if he'd let me — he's so tall and fine and splendid, when he's out among folks. All the girls are simply crazy over him. And I am, too. Only, at home — well, it's so hard to be Mary always. And you see, he named me Mary —

But I mustn't tell that here. That's part of the story, and this is only the Preface. I'm going to begin it to-morrow — the real story — Chapter One.

But, there — I mustn't call it a "chapter" out loud. Diaries don't have chapters, and this is a diary. I mustn't forget that it's a diary. But I can write it down as a chapter, for it's *going to be* a novel, after it's got done being a diary.

CHAPTER I

I Am Born

THE sun was slowly setting in the west, casting golden beams of light into the somber old room.

That 's the way it ought to begin, I know, and I 'd like to do it, but I can't. I 'm beginning with my being born, of course, and Nurse Sarah says the sun was n't shining at all. It was night and the stars were out. She remembers particularly about the stars, for Father was in the observatory, and could n't be disturbed. (We never disturb Father when he 's there, you know.) And so he did n't even know he had a daughter until the next morning when he came out to breakfast. And he was late to that, for he stopped to write down something he had found out about one of the consternations in the night.

He 's always finding out *something* about those old stars just when we want him to pay attention to something else. And, oh, I forgot to say that I know it is "constellation," and not "consternation." But I used to call them that when I was a little girl, and Mother said it was a good name for them, anyway, for they were a consternation to *her* all right. Oh, she said right off afterward that she did n't mean that, and that I must forget she said it. Mother's always saying that about things she says.

Well, as I was saying, Father did n't know until after breakfast that he had a little daughter. (We never tell him disturbing, exciting things just *before* meals.) And then Nurse told him.

I asked what he said, and Nurse laughed and gave her funny little shrug to her shoulders.

"Yes, what did he say, indeed?" she retorted. "He frowned, looked kind of dazed, then muttered: 'Well, well, upon my soul! Yes, to be sure!'"

Then he came in to see me.

I don't know, of course, what he thought of me, but I guess he did n't think much of me, from what Nurse said. Of course I was very, very small, and I never yet saw a little bit of a baby that was pretty, or looked as if it was much account. So maybe you could n't really blame him.

Nurse said he looked at me, muttered, "Well, well, upon my soul!" again, and seemed really quite interested till they started to put me in his arms. Then he threw up both hands, backed off, and cried, "Oh, no, no!" He turned to Mother and hoped she was feeling pretty well, then he got out of the room just as quick as he could. And Nurse said that was the end of it, so far as paying any more attention to me was concerned for quite a while.

He was much more interested in his new star than he was in his new daughter. We were both born the same night, you see, and that star was lots more consequence than I was. But, then, that's Father all over. And that's one of the things, I think, that bothers Mother. I heard her say once to Father that she did n't see why, when there were so many, many stars, a paltry one or two more need to be made such a fuss about. And *I* don't, either.

But Father just groaned, and shook his head, and threw up his hands, and looked *so* tired. And that's all he said. That's all he says lots of times. But it's enough. It's enough to make you feel so small and mean and insignificant as if you were just a little green worm crawling on the ground. Did you ever feel like a green worm crawling on the ground? It's not a pleasant feeling at all.

Well, now, about the name. Of course they had to begin to talk about naming me pretty soon; and Nurse said they did talk a lot. But they could n't settle it. Nurse said that that was about the first thing that showed how teetotally utterly they were going to disagree about things.

Mother wanted to call me Viola, after her mother, and Father wanted to call me Abigail Jane after his mother; and they would n't either one give in to the other. Mother was sick and nervous, and cried a lot those days, and she used to sob out that if they thought they were going to name her darling little baby that awful Abigail Jane, they were very much mistaken; that she would never give her consent to it — never. Then Father would say in his cold, stern way: "Very well, then, you need n't. But neither shall I give my consent to my daughter's being named that absurd Viola. The child is a human being — not a fiddle in an orchestra!"

And that's the way it went, Nurse said, until everybody was just about crazy. Then somebody suggested "Mary." And Father said, very well, they might call me Mary; and Mother said certainly, she would consent to Mary, only she should pronounce it Marie. And so it was settled. Father called me Mary, and Mother called me Marie. And right away everybody else began to call me Mary Marie. And that's the way it's been ever since.

Of course, when you stop to think of it, it's sort of queer and funny, though naturally I did n't think of it, growing up with it as I did, and always having it, until suddenly one day it occurred to me that none of the other girls had two names, one for their father, and one for their mother to call them by. I began to notice other things then, too. Their fathers and mothers did n't live in rooms at opposite ends of the house. Their fathers and mothers seemed to like

each other, and to talk together, and to have little jokes and laughs together, and twinkle with
their eyes. That is, most of them did.

And if one wanted to go to walk, or to a party,
or to play some game, the other did n't always
look tired and bored, and say, "Oh, very well, if
you like." And then both not do it, whatever it
was. That is, I never saw the other girls' fathers
and mothers do that way; and I've seen quite a
lot of them, too, for I've been at the other girls'
houses a lot for a long time. You see, I don't stay
at home much, only when I have to. We don't
have a round table with a red cloth and a lamp on
it, and children 'round it playing games and doing things, and fathers and mothers reading and
mending. And it 's lots jollier where they do have
them.

Nurse says my father and mother ought never
to have been married. That 's what I heard her
tell our Bridget one day. So the first chance I got
I asked her why, and what she meant.

"Oh, la! Did you hear that?" she demanded,
with the quick look over her shoulder that she
always gives when she 's talking about Father
and Mother. "Well, little pitchers do have big
ears, sure enough!"

"Little pitchers," indeed! As if I did n't know
what that meant! I 'm no child to be kept in the
dark concerning things I ought to know. And

I told her so, sweetly and pleasantly, but with firmness and dignity. I made her tell me what she meant, and I made her tell me a lot of other things about them, too. You see, I'd just decided to write the book, so I wanted to know everything she could tell me. I did n't tell her about the book, of course. I know too much to tell secrets to Nurse Sarah! But I showed my excitement and interest plainly; and when she saw how glad I was to hear everything she could tell, she talked a lot, and really seemed to enjoy it, too.

You see, she was here when Mother first came as a bride, so she knows everything. She was Father's nurse when he was a little boy; then she stayed to take care of Father's mother, Grandma Anderson, who was an invalid for a great many years and who did n't die till just after I was born. Then she took care of me. So she's always been in the family, ever since she was a young girl. She's awfully old now — 'most sixty.

First I found out how they happened to marry — Father and Mother, I'm talking about now — only Nurse says she can't see yet how they did happen to marry, just the same, they're so tee-totally different.

But this is the story.

Father went to Boston to attend a big meeting of astronomers from all over the world, and they had banquets and receptions where beautiful

ladies went in their pretty evening dresses, and
my mother was one of them. (Her father was one
of the astronomers, Nurse said.) The meetings
lasted four days, and Nurse said she guessed my
father saw a lot of my mother during that time.
Anyhow, he was invited to their home, and he
stayed another four days after the meetings were
over. The next thing they knew here at the house,
Grandma Anderson had a telegram that he was
going to be married to Miss Madge Desmond,
and would they please send him some things he
wanted, and he was going on a wedding trip and
would bring his bride home in about a month.

It was just as sudden as that. And surprising!
— Nurse says a thunderclap out of a clear blue
sky could n't have astonished them more. Father
was almost thirty years old at that time, and he'd
never cared a thing for girls, nor paid them the
least little bit of attention. So they supposed, of
course, that he was a hopeless old bachelor and
would n't ever marry. He was bound up in his
stars, even then, and was already beginning to
be famous, because of a comet he'd discovered.
He was a professor in our college here, where his
father had been president. His father had just
died a few months before, and Nurse said maybe
that was one reason why Father got caught in the
matrimonial net like that. (Those are *her* words,
not mine. The idea of calling my mother a net!

But Nurse never did half appreciate Mother.)
But Father just worshipped his father, and they
were always together — Grandma being sick so
much; and so when he died my father was nearly
beside himself, and that 's one reason they were so
anxious he should go to that meeting in Boston.
They thought it might take his mind off himself,
Nurse said. But they never thought of its putting his mind on a wife!

So far as his doing it right up quick like that
was concerned, Nurse said that was n't so surprising. For all the way up, if Father wanted
anything he insisted on having it, and having it
right away then. He never wanted to wait a minute. So when he found a girl he wanted, he wanted
her right then, without waiting a minute. He 'd
never happened to notice a girl he wanted before,
you see. But he 'd found one now, all right; and
Nurse said there was nothing to do but to make
the best of it, and get ready for her.

There was n't anybody to go to the wedding.
Grandma Anderson was sick, so of course she
could n't go, and Grandpa was dead, so of course
he could n't go, and there were n't any brothers
or sisters, only Aunt Jane in St. Paul, and she
was so mad she would n't come on. So there was
no chance of seeing the bride till Father brought
her home.

Nurse said they wondered and wondered what

kind of a woman it could be that had captured
him. (I told her I wished she *would n't* speak of
my mother as if she was some kind of a hunter
out after game; but she only chuckled and said
that's about what it amounted to in some cases.)
The very idea!

The whole town was excited over the affair,
and Nurse Sarah heard a lot of their talk. Some
thought she was an astronomer like him. Some
thought she was very rich, and maybe famous.
Everybody declared she must know a lot, anyway, and be wonderfully wise and intellectual;
and they said she was probably tall and wore
glasses, and would be thirty years old, at least.
But nobody guessed anywhere near what she
really was.

Nurse Sarah said she should never forget the
night she came, and how she looked, and how
utterly flabbergasted everybody was to see her
— a little slim eighteen-year-old girl with yellow
curly hair and the merriest laughing eyes they
had ever seen. (Don't I know? Don't I just love
Mother's eyes when they sparkle and twinkle
when we're off together sometimes in the woods?)
And Nurse said Mother was so excited the day
she came, and went laughing and dancing all
over the house, exclaiming over everything. (I
can't imagine that so well. Mother moves so
quietly now, everywhere, and is so tired, 'most

all the time.) But she was n't tired then, Nurse
says — not a mite.

"But how did Father act?" I demanded.
"Was n't he displeased and scandalized and
shocked, and everything?"

Nurse shrugged her shoulders and raised her
eyebrows — the way she does when she feels particularly superior. Then she said:

"Do? What does any old fool — beggin' your
pardon an' no offense meant, Miss Mary Marie
— but what does any man do what 's got bejug-
gled with a pretty face, an' his senses completely
took away from him by a chit of a girl? Well,
that 's what he did. He acted as if he was be-
witched. He followed her around the house like
a dog — when he was n't leadin' her to something
new; an' he never took his eyes off her face except to look at us, as much as to say: 'Now ain't
she the adorable creature?'"

"My father did that?" I gasped. And, really,
you know, I just could n't believe my ears. And
you would n't, either, if you knew Father. "Why,
I never saw him act like that!"

"No, I guess you did n't," laughed Nurse
Sarah with a shrug. "And neither did anybody
else — for long."

"But how long did it last?" I asked.

"Oh, a month, or maybe six weeks," shrugged
Nurse Sarah. "Then it came September and col-

lege began, and your father had to go back to his
teaching. Things began to change then."

"Right then, so you could see them?" I wanted
to know.

Nurse Sarah shrugged her shoulders again.

"Oh, la! child, what a little question-box you
are, an' no mistake," she sighed. But she did n't
look mad — not like the way she does when I
ask why she can take her teeth out and most of
her hair off and I can't; and things like that. (As
if I did n't know! What does she take me for — a
child?) She did n't even look displeased — Nurse
Sarah *loves* to talk. (As if I did n't know that,
too!) She just threw that quick look of hers over
her shoulder and settled back contentedly in her
chair. I knew then I should get the whole story.
And I did. And I'm going to tell it here in her
own words, just as well as I can remember it —
bad grammar and all. So please remember that I
am not making all those mistakes. It's Nurse
Sarah.

I guess, though, that I'd better put it into a
new chapter. This one is yards long already. How
do they tell when to begin and end chapters? I'm
thinking it's going to be some job, writing this
book — diary, I mean. But I shall love it, I
know. And this is a *real* story — not like those
made-up things I've always written for the girls
at school.

CHAPTER II

Nurse Sarah's Story

AND this is Nurse Sarah's story.

As I said, I'm going to tell it straight through as near as I can in her own words. And I can remember most of it, I think, for I paid very close attention.

"Well, yes, Miss Mary Marie, things did begin to change right there an' then, an' so you could notice it. *We* saw it, though maybe your pa an' ma did n't, at the first.

"You see, the first month after she came, it was vacation time, an' he could give her all the time she wanted. An' she wanted it all. An' she took it. An' he was just as glad to give it as she was to take it. An' so from mornin' till night they was together, traipsin' all over the house an' garden, an' trampin' off through the woods an' up on the mountain every other day with their lunch.

"You see she was city-bred, an' not used to woods an' flowers growin' wild; an' she went crazy over them. He showed her the stars, too, through his telescope; but she had n't a mite of use for them, an' let him see it good an' plain.

She told him — I heard her with my own ears —
that his eyes, when they laughed, was all the
stars she wanted; an' that she'd had stars all her
life for breakfast an' luncheon an' dinner, anyway, an' all the time between; an' she'd rather
have somethin' else, now — somethin' alive, that
she could love an' live with an' touch an' play
with, like she could the flowers an' rocks an'
grass an' trees.

"Angry? Your pa? Not much he was! He just
laughed an' caught her 'round the waist an'
kissed her, an' said she herself was the brightest
star of all. Then they ran off hand in hand, like
two kids. An' they *was* two kids, too. All through
those first few weeks your pa was just a great big
baby with a new plaything. Then when college
began he turned all at once into a full-grown
man. An' just naturally your ma did n't know
what to make of it.

"He could n't explore the attic an' rig up in the
old clothes there any more, nor romp through
the garden, nor go lunchin' in the woods, nor
none of the things *she* wanted him to do. He did n't
have time. An' what made things worse, one of
them comet-tails was comin' up in the sky, an'
your pa did n't take no rest for watchin' for it,
an' then studyin' of it when it got here.

"An' your ma — poor little thing! I could n't
think of anything but a doll that was thrown in

the corner because somebody'd got tired of her.
She *was* lonesome, an' no mistake. Anybody'd
be sorry for her, to see her mopin' 'round the
house, nothin' to do. Oh, she read, an' sewed
with them bright-colored silks an' worsteds; but
'course there was n't no real work for her to do.
There was good help in the kitchen, an' I took
what care of your grandma was needed; an' she
always gave her orders through me, so I practically run the house, an' there was n't anything
there for her to do.

"An' so your ma just had to mope it out alone.
Oh, I don't mean your pa was unkind. He was
always nice an' polite, when he was in the house,
an' I'm sure he meant to treat her all right. He
said yes, yes, to be sure, of course she was lonesome, an' he was sorry. 'T was too bad he was
so busy. An' he kissed her an' patted her. But he
always began right away to talk of the comet;
an' ten to one he did n't disappear into the observatory within the next five minutes. Then your
ma would look so grieved an' sorry an' go off an'
cry, an' maybe not come down to dinner, at all.

"Well, then, one day things got so bad your
grandma took a hand. She was up an' around the
house, though she kept mostly to her own rooms.
But of course she saw how things was goin'. Besides, I told her — some. 'T was no more than
my duty, as I looked at it. She just worshipped

your pa, an' naturally she'd want things right for him. So one day she told me to tell her son's wife to come to her in her room.

"An' I did, an' she came. Poor little thing! I could n't help bein' sorry for her. She did n't know a thing of what was wanted of her, an' she was so glad an' happy to come. You see, she *was* lonesome, I suppose.

"'Me? Want me? — Mother Anderson?' she cried. 'Oh, I'm so glad!' Then she made it worse by runnin' up the stairs an' bouncin' into the room like a rubber ball, an' cryin': 'Now, what shall I do, read to you, or sing to you, or shall we play games? I'd *love* to do any of them!' Just like that, she said it. I heard her. Then I went out, of course, an' left them. But I heard 'most everything that was said, just the same, for I was right in the next room dustin', and the door was n't quite shut.

"First your grandmother said real polite — she was always polite — but in a cold little voice that made even me shiver in the other room, that she did not desire to be read to or sung to, and that she did not wish to play games. She had called her daughter-in-law in to have a serious talk with her. Then she told her, still very polite, that she was noisy an' childish, an' undignified, an' that it was not only silly, but very wrong for her to expect to have her husband's entire attention;

that he had his own work, an' it was a very important one. He was going to be president of the college some day, like his father before him; an' it was her place to help him in every way she could — help him to be popular an' well-liked by all the college people an' students; an' he could n't be that if she insisted all the time on keepin' him to herself, or lookin' sour an' cross if she could n't have him.

"Of course that ain't all she said; but I remember this part particular on account of what happened afterward. You see — your ma — she felt awful bad. She cried a little, an' sighed a lot, an' said she'd try, she really would try to help her husband in every way she could; an' she would n't ask him another once, not once, to stay with her. An' she would n't look sour an' cross, either. She'd promise she would n't. An' she'd try, she'd try, oh, so hard, to be proper an' dignified.

"She got up then an' went out of the room so quiet an' still you would n't know she was movin'. But I heard her up in her room cryin' half an hour later, when I stopped a minute at her door to see if she was there. An' she was.

"But she was n't cryin' by night. Not much she was! She'd washed her face an' dressed herself up as pretty as could be, an' she never so much as looked as if she wanted her husband to stay

with her, when he said right after supper that
he guessed he'd go out to the observatory. An'
't was that way right along after that. I know,
'cause I watched. You see, I knew what she'd
said she'd do. Well, she did it.

"Then, pretty quick after that, she began to
get acquainted in the town. Folks called, an'
there was parties an' receptions where she met
folks, an' they began to come here to the house,
'specially them students, an' two or three of
them young, unmarried professors. An' she began
to go out a lot with them — skatin' an' sleigh-
ridin' an' snowshoein'.

"Like it? Of course she liked it! Who wouldn't?
Why, child, you never saw such a fuss as they
made over your ma in them days. She was all the
rage; an' of course she liked it. What woman
wouldn't, that was gay an' lively an' young, an'
had been so lonesome like your ma had? But
some other folks didn't like it. An' your pa was
one of them. This time 't was him that made the
trouble. I know, 'cause I heard what he said one
day to her in the library.

"Yes, I guess I was in the next room that day,
too — er — dustin', probably. Anyway, I heard
him tell your ma good an' plain what he thought
of her gallivantin' 'round from mornin' till night
with them young students an' professors, an'
havin' them here, too, such a lot, till the house

was fairly overrun with them. He said he was shocked an' scandalized, an' did n't she have any regard for *his* honor an' decency, if she did n't for herself! An', oh, a whole lot more.

"Cry? No, your ma did n't cry this time. I met her in the hall right after they got through talkin', an' she was white as a sheet, an' her eyes was like two blazin' stars. So I know how she must have looked while she was in the library. An' I must say she give it to him good an' plain, straight from the shoulder. She told him *she* was shocked an' scandalized that he could talk to his wife like that; an' did n't he have any more regard for *her* honor an' decency than to accuse her of runnin' after any man living — much less a dozen of them! An' then she told him a lot of what his mother had said to her, an' she said she had been merely tryin' to carry out those instructions. She was tryin' to make her husband an' her husband's wife an' her husband's home popular with the college folks, so she could help him to be president, if he wanted to be. But he answered back, cold an' chilly, that he thanked her, of course, but he did n't care for any more of that kind of assistance; an' if she would give a little more time to her home an' her housekeepin', as she ought to, he would be considerably better pleased. An' she said, very well, she would see that he had no further cause to complain. An' the next minute I met her in the hall, as I just said, her head high an' her eyes blazin'.

"An' things did change then, a lot, I'll own. Right away she began to refuse to go out with the students an' young professors, an' she sent down word she was n't to home when they called. And pretty quick, of course, they stopped comin'.

"Housekeepin'? Attend to that? Well, y-yes, she did try to at first, a little; but of course your grandma had always given the orders — through me, I mean; an' there really was n't anything your ma could do. An' I told her so, plain. Her ways were new an' different an' queer, an' we liked ours better, anyway. So she did n't bother us much that way very long. Besides, she was n't feelin' very well, anyway, an' for the next few months she stayed in her room a lot, an' we did n't see much of her. Then by an' by *you* came, an' — well, I guess that's all — too much, you little chatterbox!"

CHAPTER III

THE BREAK IS MADE

AND that's the way Nurse Sarah finished her story, only she shrugged her shoulders again, and looked back, first one way, then another. As for her calling me "chatterbox" — she always calls me that when *she's* been doing all the talking.

As near as I can remember, I have told Nurse Sarah's story exactly as she told it to me, in her own words. But of course I know I did n't get it right all the time, and I know I've left out quite a lot. But, anyway, it's told a whole lot more than *I* could have told why they got married in the first place, and it brings my story right up to the point where I was born; and I've already told about naming me, and what a time they had over that.

Of course what's happened since, up to now, I don't know *all* about, for I was only a child for the first few years. Now I'm almost a young lady, "standing with reluctant feet where the brook and river meet." (I read that last night. I think it's perfectly beautiful. So kind of sad and sweet. It makes me want to cry every time I think of it.) But even if I don't know all of what's happened

since I was born, I know a good deal, for I've
seen quite a lot, and I've made Nurse tell me a
lot more.

I know that ever since I can remember I've
had to keep as still as a mouse the minute Father
comes into the house; and I know that I never
could imagine the kind of a mother that Nurse
tells about, if it was n't that sometimes when
Father has gone off on a trip, Mother and I
have romped all over the house, and had the
most beautiful time. I know that Father says
that Mother is always trying to make me a
"Marie," and nothing else; and that Mother
says she knows Father'll never be happy until he's made me into a stupid little "Mary,"
with never an atom of life of my own. And, do
you know? it does seem sometimes, as if Mary
and Marie were fighting inside of me, and I wonder which is going to beat. Funny, is n't it?

Father is president of the college now, and I
don't know how many stars and comets and
things he's discovered since the night the star
and I were born together. But I know he's very
famous, and that he's written up in the papers
and magazines, and is in the big fat red "Who's
Who" in the library, and has lots of noted men
come to see him.

Nurse says that Grandma Anderson died very
soon after I was born, but that it did n't make

any particular difference in the housekeeping; for things went right on just as they had done, with her giving the orders as before; that she'd given them all alone anyway, mostly, the last year Grandma Anderson lived, and she knew just how Father liked things. She said Mother tried once or twice to take the reins herself, and once Nurse let her, just to see what would happen. But things got in an awful muddle right away, so that even Father noticed it and said things. After that Mother never tried again, I guess. Anyhow, she's never tried it since I can remember. She's always stayed most of the time up in her rooms in the east wing, except during meals, or when she went out with me, or went to the things she and Father had to go to together. For they did go to lots of things, Nurse says.

It seems that for a long time they did n't want folks to know there was going to be a divorce. So before folks they tried to be just as usual. But Nurse Sarah said *she* knew there was going to be one long ago. The first I ever heard of it was Nurse telling Nora, the girl we had in the kitchen then; and the minute I got a chance I asked Nurse what it was — a divorce.

My, I can remember now how scared she looked, and how she clapped her hand over my mouth. She would n't tell me — not a word. And that's the first time I ever saw her give that quick little look over each shoulder. She's done it lots of times since.

As I said, she would n't tell me, so I had to ask some one else. I was n't going to let it go by and not find out — not when Nurse Sarah looked so scared, and when it was something my father and mother were going to have some day.

I did n't like to ask Mother. Some way, I had a feeling, from the way Nurse Sarah looked, that it was something Mother was n't going to like. And I thought if maybe she did n't know yet she was going to have it, that certainly *I* did n't want to be the one to tell her. So I did n't ask Mother what a divorce was.

I did n't even think of asking Father, of course. I never ask Father questions. Nurse says I did ask him once why he did n't love me like other papas loved their little girls. But I was very little then, and I don't remember it at all. But Nurse said Father did n't like it very well, and maybe I *did* remember that part, without really knowing it. Anyhow, I never think of asking Father questions.

I asked the doctor first. I thought maybe 't was some kind of a disease, and if he knew it was coming, he could give them some sort of a medicine to keep it away — like being vaccinated so's not to have smallpox, you know. And I told him so.

He gave a funny little laugh, that somehow did n't sound like a laugh at all. Then he grew very, very sober, and said:

"I'm sorry, little girl, but I'm afraid I have n't got any medicine that will prevent — a divorce. If I did have, there'd be no eating or drinking or sleeping for me, I'm thinking — I'd be so busy answering my calls."

"Then it *is* a disease!" I cried. And I can remember just how frightened I felt. "But is n't there any doctor anywhere that *can* stop it?"

He shook his head and gave that queer little laugh again.

"I'm afraid not," he sighed. "As for it's being a disease — there are people that call it a disease, and there are others who call it a cure; and there are still others who say it's a remedy worse than the disease it tries to cure. But, there, you baby! What am I saying? Come, come, my dear, just forget it. It's nothing you should bother your little head over now. Wait till you're older."

Till I'm older, indeed! How I hate to have folks talk to me like that! And they do — they do it all the time. As if I was a child now, when I'm almost standing there where the brook and river meet!

But that was just the kind of talk I got, everywhere, nearly every time I asked any one what a divorce was. Some laughed, and some sighed.

Some looked real worried 'cause I'd asked it, and one got mad. (That was the dressmaker. I found out afterward that she'd *had* a divorce already, so probably she thought I asked the question on purpose to plague her.) But nobody would answer me — really answer me sensibly, so I'd know what it meant; and 'most everybody said, "Run away, child," or "You should n't talk of such things," or, "Wait, my dear, till you're older"; and all that.

Oh, how I hate such talk when I really want to know something! How do they expect us to get our education if they won't answer our questions?

I don't know which made me angriest — I mean angrier. (I'm speaking of two things, so I must, I suppose. I hate grammar!) To have them talk like that — not answer me, you know — or have them do as Mr. Jones, the storekeeper, did, and the men there with him.

It was one day when I was in there buying some white thread for Nurse Sarah, and it was a little while after I had asked the doctor if a divorce was a disease. Somebody had said something that made me think you could buy divorces, and I suddenly determined to ask Mr. Jones if he had them for sale. (Of course all this sounds very silly to me now, for I know that a divorce is very simple and very common. It's just like a marriage certificate, only it *un*marries you instead of marrying you; but I did n't know it then. And if I 'm going to tell this story I 've got to tell it just as it happened, of course.)

Well, I asked Mr. Jones if you could buy divorces, and if he had them for sale; and you ought to have heard those men laugh. There were six of them sitting around the stove behind me.

"Oh, yes, my little maid" (above all things I abhor to be called a little maid!) one of them cried. "You can buy them if you've got money enough; but I don't reckon our friend Jones here has got them for sale."

Then they all laughed again, and winked at each other. (That's another disgusting thing — *winks* when you ask a perfectly civil question! But what can you do? Stand it, that's all. There's such a lot of things we poor women have to stand!) Then they quieted down and looked very sober — the kind of sober you know is faced with laughs in the back — and began to tell me what a divorce really was. I can't remember them all, but I can some of them. Of course I understand now that these men were trying to be smart, and were talking for each other, not for me. And I knew it then — a little. We know a lot more things sometimes than folks think we do. Well, as near as I can remember it was like this:

"A divorce is a knife that cuts a knot that had n't ought to ever been tied," said one.

"A divorce is a jump in the dark," said another.

" No, it ain't. It's a jump from the frying pan into the fire," piped up Mr. Jones.

"A divorce is the comedy of the rich and the tragedy of the poor," said a little man who wore glasses.

"Divorce is a nice smushy poultice that may help but won't heal," cut in a new voice.

"Divorce is a guidepost marked, 'Hell to Heaven,' but lots of folks miss the way, just the same, I notice," spoke up somebody with a chuckle.

"Divorce is a coward's retreat from the battle of life." Captain Harris said this. He spoke slow and decided. Captain Harris is old and rich and not married. He's the hotel's star boarder, and what he says, goes, 'most always. But it did n't this time. I can remember just how old Mr. Carlton snapped out the next.

"Speak from your own experience, Tom Harris, an' I'm thinkin' you ain't fit ter judge. I tell you divorce is what three fourths of the husbands an' wives in the world wish was waitin' for 'em at home this very night. But it ain't there." I knew, of course, he was thinking of his wife. She's some cross, I guess, and has two warts on her nose.

There was more, quite a lot more, said. But I've forgotten the rest. Besides, they were n't talking to me then, anyway. So I picked up my thread and slipped out of the store, glad to escape. But, as I said before, I did n't find many like them.

Of course I know now — what divorce is, I mean. And it's all settled. They granted us some kind of a decree or degree, and we're going to Boston next Monday.

It's been awful, though — this last year. First we had to go to that horrid place out West, and stay ages and ages. And I hated it. Mother did, too. I know she did. I went to school, and there were quite a lot of girls my age, and some boys; but I did n't care much for them. I could n't even have the fun of surprising them with the divorce we were going to have. I found *they* were going to have one, too — every last one of them. And when everybody has a thing, you know there's no particular fun in having it yourself. Besides, they were very unkind and disagreeable, and bragged a lot about their divorces. They said mine was tame, and had no sort of snap to it, when they found Mother did n't have a lover waiting in the next town, or Father had n't run off with his stenographer, or nobody had shot anybody, or anything.

That made me mad, and I let them see it, good

and plain. I told them our divorce was perfectly all right and genteel and respectable; that Nurse Sarah said it was. Ours was going to be incompatibility, for one thing, which meant that you got on each other's nerves, and just naturally did n't care for each other any more. But they only laughed, and said even more disagreeable things, so that I did n't want to go to school any longer, and I told Mother so, and the reason, too, of course.

But, dear me, I wished right off that I had n't. I supposed she was going to be superb and haughty and disdainful, and say things that would put those girls where they belonged. But, my stars! How could I know that she was going to burst into such a storm of sobs and clasp me to her bosom, and get my face all wet and cry out: "Oh, my baby, my baby — to think I have subjected you to this, my baby, my baby!"

And I could n't say a thing to comfort her, or make her stop, even when I told her over and over again that I was n't a baby. I was almost a young lady; and I was n't being subjected to anything bad. I *liked* it — only I did n't like to have those girls brag so, when our divorce was away ahead of theirs, anyway.

But she only cried more and more, and held me tighter and tighter, rocking back and forth in her chair. She took me out of school, though, and had a lady come to teach me all by myself, so I did n't have to hear those girls brag any more, anyway. That was better. But she was n't any happier herself. I could see that.

There were lots of other ladies there — beautiful ladies — only she did n't seem to like them any better than I did the girls. I wondered if maybe *they* bragged, too, and I asked her; but she only began to cry again, and moan, "What have I done, what have I done?" — and I had to try all over again to comfort her. But I could n't.

She got so she just stayed in her room lots and lots. I tried to make her put on her pretty clothes, and do as the other ladies did, and go out and walk and sit on the big piazzas, and dance, and eat at the pretty little tables. She did, some, when we first came, and took me, and I just loved it. They were such beautiful ladies, with their bright eyes, and their red cheeks and jolly ways; and their dresses were so perfectly lovely, all silks and satins and sparkly spangles, and diamonds and rubies and emeralds, and silk stockings, and little bits of gold and silver slippers.

And once I saw two of them smoking. They had the cutest little cigarettes (Mother said they were) in gold holders, and I knew then that I was seeing life — real life; not the stupid kind you get back in a country town like Andersonville.

And I said so to Mother; and I was going to ask her if Boston was like that. But I did n't get the chance. She jumped up so quick I thought something had hurt her, and cried, "Good Heavens, Baby!" (How I hate to be called "Baby"!) Then she just threw some money on to the table to pay the bill and hurried me away.

It was after that that she began to stay in her room so much, and not take me anywhere except for walks at the other end of the town where it was all quiet and stupid, and no music or lights, or anything. And though I teased and teased to go back to the pretty, jolly places, she would n't ever take me; not once.

Then by and by, one day, we met a little black-haired woman with white cheeks and very big sad eyes. There were n't any spangly dresses and gold slippers about *her*, I can tell you! She was crying on a bench in the park, and Mother told me to stay back and watch the swans while she went up and spoke to her. (Why do old folks always make us watch swans or read books or look into store windows or run and play all the time? Don't they suppose we understand perfectly well what it means — that they 're going to say something they don't want us to hear?) Well, Mother and the lady on the bench talked and talked ever so long, and then Mother called me up, and the lady cried a little over me, and said, "Now, perhaps, if I'd had a little girl like that — !" Then she stopped and cried some more.

We saw this lady real often after that. She was nice and pretty and sweet, and I liked her; but she was always awfully sad, and I don't believe it was half so good for Mother to be with her as it would have been for her to be with those jolly, laughing ladies that were always having such good times. But I could n't make Mother see it that way at all. There are times when it seems as if Mother just *could n't* see things the way I do. Honestly, it seems sometimes almost as if *she* was the cross-current and contradiction instead of me. It does.

Well, as I said before, I did n't like it very well out there, and I don't believe Mother did, either. But it 's all over now, and we 're back home packing up to go to Boston.

Everything seems awfully queer. Maybe because Father is n't here, for one thing. He wrote very polite and asked us to come to get our things, and he said he was going to New York on business for several days, so Mother need not fear he should annoy her with his presence. Then, another thing, Mother 's queer. This morning she was singing away at the top of her voice and running all over the house picking up things she wanted; and seemed so happy. But this afternoon I found her down on the floor in the library crying as if her heart would break with her head in Father's big chair before the fireplace. But she jumped up the minute I came in and said, no, no, she did n't want anything. She was just tired; that 's all. And when I asked her if she was sorry, after all, that she was going to Boston to live, she said, no, no, no, indeed, she guessed she was n't. She was just as glad as glad could be that she was going, only she wished Monday would hurry up and come so we could be gone.

And that 's all. It 's Saturday now, and we go just day after to-morrow. Our trunks are 'most packed, and Mother says she wishes she 'd planned to go to-day. I 've said good-bye to all the girls, and promised to write loads of letters about Boston and everything. They are almost as excited as I am; and I 've promised, " cross my heart and hope to die," that I won't love those Boston girls better than I do them — specially Carrie Heywood, of course, my dearest friend.

Nurse Sarah is hovering around everywhere, asking to help, and pretending she 's sorry we 're going. But she is n't sorry. She 's glad. I know she is. She never did appreciate Mother, and she thinks she 'll have everything her own way now. But she won't. *I* could tell her a thing or two if I wanted to. But I shan't.

Father's sister, Aunt Jane Anderson, from St.

Paul, is coming to keep house for him, partly on account of Father, and partly on account of me. "If that child is going to be with her father six months of the time, she's got to have some woman there beside a meddling old nurse and a nosey servant girl!" They did n't know I heard that. But I did. And now Aunt Jane is coming. My! how mad Nurse Sarah would be if she knew. But she does n't.

I guess I'll end this chapter here and begin a fresh one down in Boston. Oh, I do so wonder what it'll be like — Boston, Mother's home, Grandpa Desmond, and all the rest. I'm so excited I can hardly wait. You see, Mother never took me home with her but once, and then I was a very small child. I don't know why, but I guess Father did n't want me to go. It's safe to say he did n't, anyway. He never wants me to do anything, hardly. That's why I suspect him of not wanting me to go down to Grandpa Desmond's. And Mother did n't go only once, in ages.

Now this will be the end. And when I begin again it will be in Boston. Only think of it — really, truly Boston!

CHAPTER IV

WHEN I AM MARIE

BOSTON.

Yes, I'm here. I've been here a week. But this is the first minute I've had a chance to write a word. I've been so busy just being here. And so has Mother. There's been such a lot going on since we came. But I'll try now to begin at the beginning and tell what happened.

Well, first we got into Boston at four o'clock Monday afternoon, and there was Grandpa Desmond to meet us. He's lovely—tall and dignified, with grayish hair and merry eyes like Mother's, only his are behind glasses. At the station he just kissed Mother and me and said he was glad to see us, and led us to the place where Peter was waiting with the car. (Peter drives Grandpa's automobile, and *he's* lovely, too.)

Mother and Grandpa talked very fast and very lively all the way home, and Mother laughed quite a lot. But in the hall she cried a little, and Grandpa patted her shoulder, and said, "There, there!" and told her how glad he was to get his little girl back, and that they were going to be very happy now and forget the past. And

Mother said, yes, yes, indeed, she knew she was; and she was *so* glad to be there, and that everything *was* going to be just the same, was n't it? Only — then, all of a sudden she looked over at me and began to cry again — only, of course, things could n't be "just the same," she choked, hurrying over to me and putting both arms around me, and crying harder than ever.

Then Grandpa came and hugged us both, and patted us, and said, "There, there!" and pulled off his glasses and wiped them very fast and very hard.

But it was n't only a minute or two before Mother was laughing again, and saying, "Nonsense!" and "The idea!" and that this was a pretty way to introduce her little Marie to her new home! Then she hurried me to the dearest little room I ever saw, right out of hers, and took off my things. Then we went all over the house. And it 's just as lovely as can be — not at all like Father's in Andersonville.

Oh, Father's is fine and big and handsome, and all that, of course; but not like this. His is just a nice place to eat and sleep in, and go to when it rains. But this — this you just want to live in all the time. Here there are curtains 'way up and sunshine, and flowers in pots, and magazines, and cozy nooks with cushions everywhere; and books that you've just been reading laid down. (*All*

Father's books are in bookcases, *always*, except while one's in your hands being read.)

Grandpa's other daughter, Mother's sister, Hattie, lives here and keeps house for Grandpa. She has a little boy named Lester, six years old; and her husband is dead. They were away for what they called a week-end when we came, but they got here a little after we did Monday afternoon; and they're lovely, too.

The house is a straight-up-and-down one with a back and front, but no sides except the one snug up to you on the right and left. And there isn't any yard except a little bit of a square brick one at the back where they have clothes and ash barrels, and a little grass spot in front at one side of the steps, not big enough for our old cat to take a nap in, hardly. But it's perfectly lovely inside; and it's the insides of houses that really count just as it is the insides of people — their hearts, I mean; whether they're good and kind, or hateful and disagreeable.

We have dinner at night here, and I've been to the theater twice already in the afternoon. I've got to go to school next week, Mother says, but so far I've just been having a good time. And so's Mother. Honestly, it has just seemed as if Mother couldn't crowd the days full enough. She hasn't been still a minute.

Lots of her old friends have been to see her;

and when there has n't been anybody else around she's taken Peter and had him drive us all over Boston to see things;—all kinds of things; Bunker Hill and museums, and moving pictures, and one play.

But we did n't stay at the play. It started out all right, but pretty soon a man and a woman on the stage began to quarrel. They were married (not really, but in the play, I mean), and I guess it was some more of that incompatibility stuff. Anyhow, as they began to talk more and more, Mother began to fidget, and pretty soon I saw she was gathering up our things; and the minute the curtain went down after the first act, she says:

"Come, dear, we're going home. It — it is n't very warm here."

As if I did n't know what she was really leaving for! Do old folks honestly think they are fooling us all the time, I wonder? But even if I had n't known then, I'd have known it later, for that evening I heard Mother and Aunt Hattie talking in the library.

No, I did n't listen. I *heard*. And that's a very different matter. You listen when you mean to, and that's sneaking. You hear when you can't help yourself, and that you can't be blamed for. Sometimes it's your good luck, and sometimes it's your bad luck — just according to what you hear!

Well, I was in the window-seat in the library reading when Mother and Aunt Hattie came in; and Mother was saying:

"Of course I came out! Do you suppose I'd have had that child see that play, after I realized what it was? As if she hasn't had enough of such wretched stuff already in her short life! Oh, Hattie, Hattie, I want that child to laugh, to sing, to fairly tingle with the joy of living every minute that she is with me. I know so well what she *has* had, and what she will have — in that — tomb. You know in six months she goes back — "

Mother saw me then, I know; for she stopped right off short, and after a moment began to talk of something else, very fast. And pretty quick they went out into the hall again.

Dear little Mother! Bless her old heart! Isn't she the ducky dear to want me to have all the good times possible now so as to make up for the six months I've got to be with Father? You see, she knows what it is to live with Father even better than I do.

Well, I guess she doesn't dread it for me any more than I do for myself. Still, I'll have the girls there, and I'm dying to see them again — and I won't have to stay home much, only nights and meals, of course, and Father's always pretty busy with his stars and comets and things.

Besides, it's only for six months, then I can come back to Boston. I can keep thinking of that.

But I know now why I've been having such a perfectly beautiful time all this week, and why Mother has been filling every minute so full of fun and good times. Why, even when we're at home here, she's always hunting up little Lester and getting him to have a romp with us.

But of course next week I've got to go to school, and it can't be quite so jolly then. Well, I guess that's all for this time.

About a month later.

I did n't make a chapter of that last. It was n't long enough. And, really, I don't know as I've got much to add to it now. There's nothing much happened.

I go to school now, and don't have so much time for fun. School is pretty good, and there are two or three girls 'most as nice as the ones at Andersonville. But not quite. Out of school Mother keeps things just as lively as ever, and we have beautiful times. Mother is having a lovely time with her own friends, too. Seems as if there is always some one here when I get home, and lots of times there are teas and parties, and people to dinner.

There are gentlemen, too. I suppose one of

them will be Mother's lover by and by; but of
course I don't know which one yet. I'm awfully
interested in them, though. And of course it's
perfectly natural that I should be. Would n't *you*
be interested in the man that was going to be
your new father? Well, I just guess you would!
Anybody would. Why, most folks have only one
father, you know, and they have to take that one
just as he is; and it's all a matter of chance
whether they get one that's cross or pleasant; or
homely or fine and grand-looking; or the common kind you can hug and kiss and hang round
his neck, or the stand-off-don't-touch-me-I-
must n't-be-disturbed kind like mine. I mean the
one I *did* have. But, there! that does n't sound
right, either; for of course he's still my father
just the same, only — well, he is n't Mother's
husband any more, so I suppose he's only my
father by order of the court, same as I'm his
daughter.

Well, anyhow, he's the father I've grown up
with, and of course I'm used to him now. And
it's an altogether different matter to think of
having a brand-new father thrust upon you, all
ready-made, as you might say, and of course I *am*
interested. There's such a whole lot depends on
the father. Why, only think how different things
would have been at home if *my* father had been
different! There were such a lot of things I had to

be careful not to do — and just as many I had to
be careful *to* do — on account of Father.

And so now, when I see all these nice young
gentlemen (only they are n't all young; some of
them are quite old) coming to the house and
talking to Mother, and hanging over the back of
her chair, and handing her tea and little cakes, I
can't help wondering which, if any, is going to be
her lover and my new father. And I am also wondering what I'll have to do on account of him
when I get him, if I get him.

There are quite a lot of them, and they're all
different. They'd make very different kinds of
fathers, I'm sure, and I'm afraid I would n't like
some of them. But, after all, it's Mother that
ought to settle which to have — not me. *She's* the
one to be pleased. 'T would be such a pity to have
to change again. Though she could, of course,
same as she did Father, I suppose.

As I said, they're all different. There are only
two that are anywhere near alike, and they are n't
quite the same, for one's a lawyer and the other's
in a bank. But they both carry canes and wear
tall silk hats, and part their hair in the middle,
and look at you through the kind of big round
eyeglasses with dark rims that would make you
look awfully homely if they did n't make you
look so stylish. But I don't think Mother cares
very much for either the lawyer or the bank man,

and I'm glad. I would n't like to live with those
glasses every day, even if they are stylish. I'd
much rather have Father's kind.

Then there's the man that paints pictures.
He's tall and slim, and wears queer ties and long
hair. He's always standing back and looking at
things with his head on one side, and exclaiming
"Oh!" and "Ah!" with a long breath. He says
Mother's coloring is wonderful. I heard him. And
I did n't like it very well, either. Why, it sounded
as if she put it on herself out of a box on her
bureau, same as some other ladies do! Still, he's
not so bad, maybe; though I'm not sure but what
his paints and pictures would be just as tiresome
to live with as Father's stars, when it came right
down to wanting a husband to live with you and
talk to you every day in the year. You know you
have to think of such things when it comes to
choosing a new father — I mean a new husband.
(I keep forgetting that it's Mother and not me
that's doing the choosing.)

Well, to resume and go on. There's the violinist. I must n't forget him. But, then, nobody
could forget him. He's lovely: so handsome and
distinguished-looking with his perfectly beautiful dark eyes and white teeth. And he plays —
well, I'm simply crazy over his playing. I only
wish Carrie Heywood could hear him. She thinks
her brother can play. He's a traveling violinist

with a show; and he came home once to Andersonville. And I heard him. But he's not the real
thing at all. Not a bit. Why, he might be anybody,
our grocer, or the butcher, up there playing that
violin. His eyes are little and blue, and his hair is
red and very short. I wish she could hear *our*
violinist play!

And there's another man that comes to the
parties and teas; — oh, of course there are others,
lots of them, married men with wives, and unmarried men with and without sisters. But I
mean another man specially. His name is Harlow.
He's a little man with a brown pointed beard and
big soft brown eyes. He's really awfully good-
looking, too. I don't know what he does do; but
he's married. I know that. He never brings his
wife, though; but Mother's always asking for her,
clear and distinct, and she always smiles, and her
voice kind of tinkles like little silver bells. But
just the same he never brings her.

He never takes her anywhere. I heard Aunt
Hattie tell Mother so at the very first, when he
came. She said they were n't a bit happy together,
and that there'd probably be a divorce before
long. But Mother asked for her just the same the
very next time. And she's done it ever since.

I think I know now why she does. I found out,
and I was simply thrilled. It was so exciting! You
see, they were lovers once themselves — Mother

and this Mr. Harlow. Then something happened and they quarreled. That was just before Father came.

Of course Mother did n't tell me this, nor Aunt Hattie. It was two ladies. I heard them talking at a tea one day. I was right behind them, and I could n't get away, so I just could n't help hearing what they said.

They were looking across the room at Mother. Mr. Harlow was talking to her. He was leaning forward in his chair and talking so earnestly to Mother; and he looked just as if he thought there was n't another soul in the room but just they two. But Mother — Mother was just listening to be polite to company. Anybody could see that. And the very first chance she got she turned and began to talk to a lady who was standing near. And she never so much as looked toward Mr. Harlow again.

The ladies in front of me laughed then, and one of them said, with a little nod of her head, "I guess Madge Desmond Anderson can look out for herself all right."

Then they got up and went away without seeing me. And all of a sudden I felt almost sorry, for I wanted them to see me. I wanted them to see that I knew my mother could take care of herself, too, and that I was proud of it. If they had turned I'd have said so. But they did n't turn.

I should n't like Mr. Harlow for a father. I
know I should n't. But then, there's no danger,
of course, even if he and Mother were lovers
once. He's got a wife now, and even if he got a
divorce, I don't believe Mother would choose him.

But of course there's no telling which one she
will take. As I said before, I don't know. It's too
soon, anyway, to tell. I suspect it is n't any more
proper to hurry up about getting married again
when you've been *un*married by a divorce than
it is when you've been unmarried by your husband's dying. I asked Peter one day how soon
folks did get married after a divorce, but he
did n't seem to know. Anyway, all he said was to
stammer: "Er — yes, Miss — no, Miss. I mean,
I don't know, Miss."

Peter is awfully funny. But he's nice. I like
him, only I can't find out much by him. He's
very good-looking, though he's quite old. He's
almost thirty. He told me. I asked him. He takes
me back and forth to school every day, so I see
quite a lot of him. And, really, he's about the
only one I *can* ask questions of here, anyway.
There is n't anybody like Nurse Sarah used to be.
Olga, the cook, talks so funny I can't understand
a word she says, hardly. Besides, the only two
times I've been down to the kitchen Aunt Hattie sent for me; and she told me the last time
not to go any more. She did n't say why. Aunt

Hattie never says *why* not to do things. She just
says, " Don't." Sometimes it seems to me as if
my whole life had been made up of "don'ts."
If they'd only tell us part of the time things to
"*do*," maybe we wouldn't have so much time
to do the "*don'ts.*" (That sounds funny, but I
guess folks'll know what I mean.)

Well, what was I saying? Oh, I know —
about asking questions. As I said, there isn't
anybody like Nurse Sarah here. I can't understand Olga, and Theresa, the other maid, is just
about as bad. Aunt Hattie's lovely, but I can't
ask questions of her. She isn't the kind. Besides,
Lester's always there, too; and you can't discuss
family affairs before children. Of course there's
Mother and Grandpa Desmond. But questions
like when it's proper for Mother to have lovers
I can't ask of *them*, of course. So there's no one
but Peter left to ask. Peter's all right and very
nice, but he doesn't seem to know *anything* that
I want to know. So he doesn't amount to so very
much, after all.

I'm not sure, anyway, that Mother'll want to
get married again. From little things she says I
rather guess she doesn't think much of marriage,
anyway. One day I heard her say to Aunt Hattie
that it was a very pretty theory that marriages
were made in heaven, but that the real facts of
the case were that they were made on earth. And

another day I heard her say that one trouble with marriage was that the husband and wife did n't know how to play together and to rest together. And lots of times I 've heard her say little things to Aunt Hattie that showed how unhappy *her* marriage had been.

But last night a funny thing happened. We were all in the library reading after dinner, and Grandpa looked up from his paper and said something about a woman that was sentenced to be hanged and how a whole lot of men were writing letters protesting against having a woman hanged; but there were only one or two letters from women. And Grandpa said that only went to prove how much more lacking in a sense of fitness of things women were than men. And he was just going to say more when Aunt Hattie bristled up and tossed her chin, and said, real indignantly:

"A sense of fitness of things, indeed! Oh, yes, that 's all very well to say. There are plenty of men, no doubt, who are shocked beyond anything at the idea of hanging a woman; but those same men will think nothing of going straight home and making life for some other woman so absolutely miserable that she 'd think hanging would be a lucky escape from something worse."

"Harriet!" exclaimed Grandpa in a shocked voice.

"Well, I mean it!" declared Aunt Hattie emphatically. "Look at poor Madge here, and that wretch of a husband of hers!"

And just here is where the funny thing happened. Mother bristled up — *Mother* — and even more than Aunt Hattie had. She turned red and then white, and her eyes blazed.

"That will do, Hattie, please, in my presence," she said, very cold, like ice. " Dr. Anderson is not a wretch at all. He is an honorable, scholarly gentleman. Without doubt he meant to be kind and considerate. He simply did not understand me. We were n't suited to each other. That 's all."

And she got up and swept out of the room.

Now was n't that funny? But I just loved it, all the same. I always love Mother when she 's superb and haughty and disdainful.

Well, after she had gone Aunt Hattie looked at Grandpa and Grandpa looked at Aunt Hattie. Grandpa shrugged his shoulders, and gave his hands a funny little flourish; and Aunt Hattie lifted her eyebrows and said:

"Well, what do you know about that?" (Aunt Hattie forgot I was in the room, I know, or she 'd never in the world have used slang like that!) "And after all the things she 's said about how unhappy she was!" finished Aunt Hattie.

Grandpa did n't say anything, but just gave his funny little shrug again.

And it was kind of queer, when you come to think of it — about Mother, I mean, was n't it?

One month later.

Well, I've been here another whole month, and it's growing nicer all the time. I just love it here. I love the sunshine everywhere, and the curtains up to let it in. And the flowers in the rooms, and the little fern-dish on the dining-room table, the books and magazines just lying around ready to be picked up; Baby Lester laughing and singing all over the house, and lovely ladies and gentlemen in the drawing-room having music and tea and little cakes when I come home from school in the afternoon. And I love it not to have to look up and watch and listen for fear Father's coming in and I'll be making a noise. And best of all I love Mother with her dancing eyes and her laugh, and her just being happy, with no going in and finding her crying or looking long and fixedly at nothing, and then turning to me with a great big sigh, and a "Well, dear?" that just makes you want to go and cry because it's so hurt and heart-broken. Oh, I do just love it all!

And Mother *is* happy. I'm sure she is. Somebody is doing something for her every moment — seems so. They are so glad to get her back again. I know they are. I heard two ladies talking one day, and they said they were. They called

her "Poor Madge," and "Dear Madge," and
they said it was a shame that she should have
had such a wretched experience, and that they
for one should try to do everything they could to
make her forget.

And that's what they all seem to be trying to
do — to make her forget. There is n't a day goes
by but that somebody sends flowers or books or
candy, or invites her somewhere, or takes her to
ride or to the theater, or comes to see her, so that
Mother is in just one whirl of good times from
morning till night. Why, she'd just have to forget.
She does n't have any time to remember. I think
she *is* forgetting, too. Oh, of course she gets tired,
and sometimes rainy days or twilights I find her
on the sofa in her room not reading or anything,
and her face looks 'most as it used to sometimes
after they'd been having one of their incompatibility times. But I don't find her that way very
often, and it does n't last long. So I really think
she is forgetting.

About the prospective suitors — I found that
"prospective suitor" in a story a week ago, and
I just love it. It means you probably will want
to marry her, you know. I use it all the time now
— in my mind — when I'm thinking about those
gentlemen that come here (the unmarried ones).
I forgot and used it out loud one day to Aunt
Hattie; but I shan't again. She said, "Mercy!"

and threw up her hands and looked over to
Grandpa the way she does when I've said something she thinks is perfectly awful.

But I was firm and dignified — but very polite and pleasant — and I said that I did n't see
why she should act like that, for of course they
were prospective suitors, the unmarried ones,
anyway, and even some of the married ones,
maybe, like Mr. Harlow, for of course they could
get divorces, and —

"*Marie!*" interrupted Aunt Hattie then, before I could say another word, or go on to explain
that of course Mother could n't be expected to
stay unmarried *always*, though I was very sure
she would n't get married again until she'd
waited long enough, and until it was perfectly
proper and genteel for her to take unto herself
another husband.

But Aunt Hattie would n't even listen. And
she threw up her hands and said "*Marie!*" again
with the emphasis on the last part of the name
the way I simply loathe. And she told me never,
never to let her hear me make such a speech as
that again. And I said I would be very careful
not to. And you may be sure I shall. I don't want
to go through a scene like that again!

She told Mother about it, though, I think. Anyhow, they were talking very busily together when
they came into the library after dinner that night,

and Mother looked sort of flushed and plagued,
and I heard her say, "Perhaps the child does read
too many novels, Hattie."

And Aunt Hattie answered, "Of course she
does!" Then she said something else which I did
n't catch, only the words "silly" and "romantic" and "pre-co-shus." (I don't know what that
last means, but I put it down the way it sounded,
and I'm going to look it up.)

Then they turned and saw me, and they did
n't say anything more. But the next morning the
perfectly lovely story I was reading, that Theresa let me take, called "The Hidden Secret,"
I could n't find anywhere. And when I asked
Mother if she'd seen it, she said she'd given it
back to Theresa, and that I must n't ask for
it again. That I was n't old enough yet to read
such stories.

There it is again! I'm not old enough. When
will I be allowed to take my proper place in life?
Echo answers when.

Well, to resume and go on.

What was I talking about? Oh, I know — the
prospective suitors. (Aunt Hattie can't hear me
when I just *write* it, anyway.) Well, they all come
just as they used to, only there are more of them
now — two fat men, one slim one, and a man
with a halo of hair round a bald spot. Oh, I don't
mean that any of them are really suitors yet.

They just come to call and to tea, and send her
flowers and candy. And Mother is n't a mite
nicer to one than she is to any of the others. Anybody can see that. And she shows very plainly
she's no notion of picking anybody out yet.
But of course I can't help being interested and
watching.

It won't be Mr. Harlow, anyway. I'm pretty
sure of that, even if he has started in to get his
divorce. (And he has. I heard Aunt Hattie tell
Mother so last week.) But Mother does n't like
him. I'm sure she does n't. He makes her awfully
nervous. Oh, she laughs and talks with him —
seems as if she laughs even more with him than
she does with anybody else. But she's always
looking around for somebody else to talk to; and
I've seen her get up and move off just as he was
coming across the room toward her, and I'm just
sure she saw him. There's another reason, too,
why I think Mother is n't going to choose him
for her lover. I heard something she said to him
one day.

She was sitting before the fire in the library,
and he came in. There were other people there,
quite a lot of them; but Mother was all alone by
the fireplace, her eyes looking fixed and dreamy
into the fire. I was in the window-seat around the
corner of the chimney reading; and I could see
Mother in the mirror just as plain as could be.

She could have seen me, too, of course, if she'd looked up. But she did n't.

I never even thought of hearing anything I had n't ought, and I was just going to get down to go and speak to Mother myself, when Mr. Harlow crossed the room and sat down on the sofa beside her.

"Dreaming, Madge?" he said, low and soft, his soulful eyes just devouring her lovely face. (I read that, too, in a book last week. I just loved it!)

Mother started and flushed up.

"Oh, Mr. Harlow!" she cried. (Mother always calls him "Mr." That's another thing. He always calls her "Madge," you know.) "How do you do?" Then she gave her quick little look around to see if there was n't somebody else near for her to talk to. But there was n't.

" But you *do* dream of the old days, sometimes, Madge, don't you?" he began again, soft and low, leaning a little nearer.

"Of when I was a child and played dolls before this very fireplace? Well, yes, perhaps I do," laughed Mother. And I could see she drew away a little. "There was one doll with a broken head that —"

"*I* was speaking of broken hearts," interrupted Mr. Harlow, very meaningfully.

"Broken hearts! Nonsense! As if there were

such things in the world!" cried Mother, with a little toss to her head, looking around again with a quick little glance for some one else to talk to.

But still there was n't anybody there.

They were all over to the other side of the room talking, and paying no attention to Mother and Mr. Harlow, only the violinist. He looked and looked, and acted nervous with his watch-chain. But he did n't come over. I felt, some way, that I ought to go away and not hear any more; but I could n't without showing them that I had been there. So I thought it was better to stay just where I was. They could see me, anyway, if they 'd just look in the mirror. So I did n't feel that I was sneaking. And I stayed.

Then Mr. Harlow spoke again. His eyes grew even more soulful and devouring. I could see them in the mirror.

"Madge, it seems so strange that we should both have had to trail through the tragedy of broken hearts and lives before we came to our real happiness. For we *shall* be happy, Madge. You know I 'm to be free, too, soon, dear, and then we —"

But he did n't finish. Mother put up her hand and stopped him. Her face was n't flushed any more. It was very white.

"Carl," she began in a still, quiet voice, and I was so thrilled. I knew something was going to

happen — this time she'd called him by his first
name. "I'm sorry," she went on. "I've tried to
show you. I've tried very hard to show you —
without speaking. But if you make me say it I
shall have to say it. Whether you are free or not
matters not to me. It can make no difference in
our relationship. Now, will you come with me to
the other side of the room, or must I be so rude
as to go and leave you?"

She got up then, and he got up, too. He said
something — I could n't hear what it was; but
it was sad and reproachful — I'm sure of that
by the look in his eyes. Then they both walked
across the room to the others.

I was sorry for him. I do not want him for a
father, but I could n't help being sorry for him,
he looked so sad and mournful and handsome;
and he's got perfectly beautiful eyes. (Oh, I do
hope mine will have nice eyes, when I find him!)

As I said before, I don't believe Mother'll
choose Mr. Harlow, anyway, even when the time
comes. As for any of the others — I can't tell.
She treats them all just exactly alike, as far as I
can see. Polite and pleasant, but not at all lover-
like. I was talking to Peter one day about it, and
I asked him. But he did n't seem to know, either,
which one she will be likely to take, if any.

Peter's about the only one I can ask. Of course
I could n't ask Mother, or Aunt Hattie, after

what *she* said about my calling them prospective
suitors. And Grandfather — well, I should never
think of asking Grandpa a question like that.
But Peter — Peter's a real comfort. I'm sure I
don't know what I should do for somebody to
talk to and ask questions about things down here,
if it was n't for him. As I think I've said already,
he takes me to school and back again every day;
so of course I see him quite a lot.

Speaking of school, it's all right, and of course
I like it, though not quite so well as I did. There
are some of the girls — well, they act queer. I
don't know what is the matter with them. They
stop talking — some of them — when I come up,
and they make me feel, sometimes, as if I did n't
belong. Maybe it's because I came from a little
country town like Andersonville. But they've
known that all along, from the very first. And
they did n't act at all like that at the beginning.
Maybe it's just their way down here. If I think
of it I'll ask Peter to-morrow.

Well, I guess that's all I can think of this time.

'Most four months later.

It's been ages since I've written here, I know.
But there's nothing special happened. Everything has been going along just about as it did
at the first. Oh, there is one thing different —
Peter's gone. He went two months ago. We've

got an awfully old chauffeur now. One with gray
hair and glasses, and homely, too. His name is
Charles. The very first day he came, Aunt Hattie
told me never to talk to Charles, or bother him
with questions; that it was better he should keep
his mind entirely on his driving.

She need n't have worried. I should never
dream of asking him the things I did Peter. He 's
too stupid. Now Peter and I got to be real good
friends — until all of a sudden Grandpa told him
he might go. I don't know why.

I don't see as I'm any nearer finding out who
Mother's lover will be than I was four months
ago. I suppose it 's still too soon. Peter said one
day he thought widows ought to wait at least a
year, and he guessed grass-widows were just the
same. My, how mad I was at him for using that
name about my mother! Oh, I knew what he
meant. I'd heard it at school. (I know now what
it was that made those girls act so queer and horrid.) There was a girl — I never liked her, and
I suspect she did n't like me, either. Well, she
found out Mother had a divorce. (You see, I
had n't told it. I remembered how those girls
out West bragged.) And she told a lot of the
others. But it did n't work at all as it had in the
West. None of the girls in this school here had a
divorce in their families; and, if you 'll believe it,
they acted — some of them — as if it was a *dis-*

grace, even after I told them good and plain that ours was a perfectly respectable and genteel divorce. Nothing I could say made a mite of difference, with some of the girls, and then is when I first heard that perfectly horrid word, "grass-widow." So I knew what Peter meant, though I was furious at him for using it. And I let him see it good and plain.

Of course I changed schools. I knew Mother'd want me to, when she knew, and so I told her right away. I thought she'd be superb and haughty and disdainful sure this time. But she was n't. First she grew so white I thought she was going to faint away. Then she began to cry, and kiss and hug me. And that night I heard her talking to Aunt Hattie and saying, "To think that that poor innocent child has to suffer, too!" and some more which I could n't hear, because her voice was all choked up and shaky.

Mother is crying now again quite a lot. You see, her six months are 'most up, and I've got to go back to Father. And I'm afraid Mother is awfully unhappy about it. She had a letter last week from Aunt Jane, Father's sister. I heard her read it out loud to Aunt Hattie and Grandpa in the library. It was very stiff and cold and dignified, and ran something like this:

DEAR MADAM: Dr. Anderson desires me to say that he trusts you are bearing in mind the fact that, according to the decision of the court, his daughter Mary is to come to him on the first day of May. If you will kindly inform him as to the hour of her expected arrival, he will see that she is properly met at the station.

Then she signed her name, Abigail Jane Anderson. (She was named for her mother, Grandma Anderson, same as Father wanted them to name me. Mercy! I'm glad they didn't. "Mary" is bad enough, but "Abigail Jane" —!)

Well, Mother read the letter aloud, then she began to talk about it — how she felt, and how awful it was to think of giving me up six whole months, and sending her bright little sunny-hearted Marie into that tomb-like place with only an Abigail Jane to flee to for refuge. And she said that she almost wished Nurse Sarah was back again — that she, at least, was human.

"'And see that she's properly met,' indeed!" went on Mother, with an indignant little choke in her voice. "Oh, yes, I know! Now if it were a star or a comet that he expected, he'd go himself and sit for hours and hours watching for it. But when his daughter comes, he'll send John with the horses, like enough, and possibly that precious Abigail Jane of his. Or, maybe that is too much to expect. Oh, Hattie, I can't let her go — I can't, I can't!"

I was in the window-seat around the corner

of the chimney, reading; and I don't know as she knew I was there. But I was, and I heard. And I've heard other things, too, all this week.

I'm to go next Monday, and as it comes nearer the time Mother's getting worse and worse. She's so unhappy over it. And of course that makes me unhappy, too. But I try not to show it. Only yesterday, when she was crying and hugging me, and telling me how awful it was that her little girl should have to suffer, too, I told her not to worry a bit about me; that I wasn't suffering at all. I *liked* it. It was ever so much more exciting to have two homes instead of one. But she only cried all the more, and sobbed, "Oh, my baby, my baby!" — so nothing I could say seemed to do one mite of good.

But I meant it, and I told the truth. I *am* excited. And I can't help wondering how it's all going to be at Father's. Oh, of course, I know it won't be so much fun, and I'll have to be "Mary," and all that; but it'll be something *different*, and I always did like different things. Besides, there's Father's love story to watch. Maybe *he's* found somebody. Maybe he didn't wait a year. Anyhow, if he did find somebody I'm sure he wouldn't be so willing to wait as Mother would. You know Nurse Sarah said Father never wanted to wait for anything. That's why he married Mother so quick, in the first place. But if there is

"I TOLD HER NOT TO WORRY A BIT ABOUT ME"

somebody, of course I'll find out when I'm there.
So that'll be interesting. And, anyway, there'll
be the girls. I shall have *them*.

I'll close now, and make this the end of the
chapter. It'll be Andersonville next time.

CHAPTER V

When I am Mary

Andersonville.

Well, here I am. I've been here two days now, and I guess I'd better write down what's happened so far, before I forget it.

First, about my leaving Boston. Poor, dear Mother did take on dreadfully, and I thought she just would n't let me go. She went with me to the junction where I had to change, and put me on the parlor car for Andersonville, and asked the conductor to look out for me. (As if I needed that — a young lady like me! I'm fourteen now. I had a birthday last week.)

But I thought at the last that she just would n't let me go, she clung to me so, and begged me to forgive her for all she'd brought upon me; and said it was a cruel, cruel shame, when there were children, and people ought to stop and think and remember, and be willing to stand anything. And then, in the next breath, she'd beg me not to forget her, and not to love Father better than I did her. (As if there was any danger of that!) And to write to her every few minutes.

Then the conductor cried, "All aboard!" and the bell rang, and she had to go and leave me.

But the last I saw of her she was waving her handkerchief, and smiling the kind of a smile that's
worse than crying right out loud. Mother's
always like that. No matter how bad she feels,
at the last minute she comes up bright and smiling, and just as brave as can be.

I had a wonderful trip to Andersonville. Everybody was very kind to me, and there were lovely
things to see out the window. The conductor came
in and spoke to me several times — not the way
you would look after a child, but the way a gentleman would tend to a lady. I liked him very
much.

There was a young gentleman in the seat in
front, too, who was very nice. He loaned me a magazine, and bought some candy for me; but I did
n't see much more of him, for the second time the
conductor came in he told me he'd found a nice
seat back in the car on the shady side. He noticed
the sun came in where I sat, he said. (*I* had n't
noticed it specially.) But he picked up my bag
and magazine — but I guess he forgot the candy-
box the nice young gentleman in front had just
put on my window-sill, for when I got into my
new seat the candy was n't anywhere; and of
course I did n't like to go back for it. But the
conductor was very nice and kind, and came in
twice again to see if I liked my new seat; and of
course I said I did. It was very nice and shady,

and there was a lady and a baby in the next seat, and I played with the baby quite a lot.

It was heaps of fun to be grown up and traveling alone like that! I sat back in my seat and wondered and wondered what the next six months were going to be like. And I wondered, too, if I'd forgotten how to be "Mary."

"Dear me! How shall I ever remember not to run and skip and laugh loud or sing, or ask questions, or do *anything* that Marie wants to do?" I thought to myself.

And I wondered if Aunt Jane would meet me, and what she would be like. She came once when I was a little girl, Mother said; but I did n't remember her.

Well, at last we got to Andersonville. John was there with the horses, and Aunt Jane, too. Of course I knew she must be Aunt Jane, because she was with John. The conductor was awfully nice and polite, and did n't leave me till he'd seen me safe in the hands of Aunt Jane and John. Then he went back to his train, and the next minute it had whizzed out of the station, and I was alone with the beginning of my next six months.

The first beginning was a nice smile, and a "Glad to see ye home, Miss," from John, as he touched his hat, and the next was a "How do you do, Mary?" from Aunt Jane. And I knew right off that first minute that I was n't going to like Aunt Jane — just the way she said that "Mary," and the way she looked me over from head to foot.

Aunt Jane is tall and thin, and wears black — not the pretty, stylish black, but the "I-don't-care" rusty black — and a stiff white collar. Her eyes are the kind that says, "I'm surprised at you!" all the time, and her mouth is the kind that never shows any teeth when it smiles, and does n't smile much, anyway. Her hair is some gray, and does n't kink or curl anywhere; and I knew right off the first minute she looked at me that she did n't like mine, 'cause it did curl.

I was pretty sure she did n't like my clothes, either. I've since found out she did n't — but more of that anon. (I just love that word "anon.") And I just knew she disapproved of my hat. But she did n't say anything — not in words — and after we'd attended to my trunk, we went along to the carriage and got in.

My stars! I did n't suppose horses *could* go so slow. Why, we were *ages* just going a block. You see I'd forgotten; and without thinking I spoke right out.

"My! Horses *are* slow, are n't they?" I cried. "You see, Grandpa has an auto, and —"

"Mary!" — just like that she interrupted —

Aunt Jane did. (Funny how old folks can do what they won't let you do. Now if I'd interrupted anybody like that!) "You may as well understand at once," went on Aunt Jane, "that we are not interested in your grandfather's auto, or his house, or anything that is his." (I felt as if I was hearing the catechism in church!) "And that the less reference you make to your life in Boston, the better we shall be pleased. As I said before, we are not interested. Besides, while under your father's roof, it would seem to me very poor taste, indeed, for you to make constant reference to things you may have been doing while *not* under his roof. The situation is deplorable enough, however you take it, without making it positively unbearable. You will remember, Mary?"

Mary said, "Yes, Aunt Jane," very polite and proper; but I can tell you that inside of Mary, *Marie* was just boiling.

Unbearable, indeed!

We did n't say anything more all the way home. Naturally, *I* was not going to, after that speech; and Aunt Jane said nothing. So silence reigned supreme.

Then we got home. Things looked quite natural, only there was a new maid in the kitchen, and Nurse Sarah was n't there. Father was n't there, either. And, just as I suspected, 't was a star that was to blame, only this time the star was the moon — an eclipse; and he'd gone somewhere out West so he could see it better.

He is n't coming back till next week; and when I think how he made me come on the first day, so as to get in the whole six months, when all the time he did not care enough about it to be here himself, I'm just mad — I mean, the righteously indignant kind of mad — for I can't help thinking how poor Mother would have loved those extra days with her.

Aunt Jane said I was to have my old room, and so, as soon as I got here, I went right up and took off my hat and coat, and pretty quick they brought up my trunk, and I unpacked it; and I did n't hurry about it either. I was n't a bit anxious to get downstairs again to Aunt Jane. Besides, I may as well own up, I was crying — a little. Mother's room was right across the hall, and it looked so lonesome; and I could n't help remembering how different this homecoming was from the one in Boston, six months ago.

Well, at last I had to go down to dinner — I mean supper — and, by the way, I made another break on that. I *called* it dinner right out loud, and never thought — till I saw Aunt Jane's face.

"*Supper* will be ready directly," she said, with cold and icy emphasis. "And may I ask you to remember, Mary, please, that Andersonville has dinner at *noon*, not at six o'clock."

"Yes, Aunt Jane," said Mary, polite and proper again. (I shan't say what Marie said inside.)

We did n't do anything in the evening but read and go to bed at nine o'clock. I *wanted* to run over to Carrie Heywood's; but Aunt Jane said no, not till morning. (I wonder why young folks *never* can do things when they *want* to do them, but must always wait till morning or night or noon, or some other time!)

In the morning I went up to the schoolhouse. I planned it so as to get there at recess, and I saw all the girls except one that was sick, and one that was away. We had a perfectly lovely time, only everybody was talking at once so that I don't know now what was said. But they seemed glad to see me. I know that. Maybe I 'll go to school next week. Aunt Jane says she thinks I ought to, when it 's only the first of May. She 's going to speak to Father when he comes next week.

She was going to speak to him about my clothes; then she decided to attend to those herself, and not bother him. As I suspected, she does n't like my dresses. I found out this morning for sure. She came into my room and asked to see my things. My! But did n't I hate to show them to her? Marie said she would n't; but Mary obediently trotted to the closet and brought them out one by one.

Aunt Jane turned them around with the tips of her fingers, all the time sighing and shaking her head. When I'd brought them all out, she shook her head again and said they would not do at all — not in Andersonville; that they were extravagant, and much too elaborate for a young girl; that she would see the dressmaker and arrange that I had some serviceable blue and brown serges at once.

Blue and brown serge, indeed! But, there, what's the use? I'm Mary now. I keep forgetting that; though I don't see how I can forget it — with Aunt Jane around.

But, listen. A funny thing happened this morning. Something came up about Boston, and Aunt Jane asked me a question. Then she asked another and another, and she kept me talking till I guess I talked 'most a whole half-hour about Grandpa Desmond, Aunt Hattie, Mother, and the house, and what we did, and, oh, a whole lot of things. And here, just two days ago, she was telling me that she was n't interested in Grandpa Desmond, his home, or his daughter, or anything that was his!

There's something funny about Aunt Jane.

One week later.

Father's come. He came yesterday. But I did n't know it, and I came running downstairs,

ending with a little bounce for the last step. And
there, right in front of me in the hall was —
Father.

I guess he was as much surprised as I was.
Anyhow, he acted so. He just stood stock-still
and stared, his face turning all kinds of colors.

"You?" he gasped, just above his breath.
Then suddenly he seemed to remember. "Why,
yes, yes, to be sure. You are here, are n't you?
How do you do, Mary?"

He came up then and held out his hand, and
I thought that was all he was going to do. But
after a funny little hesitation he stooped and
kissed my forehead. Then he turned and went
into the library with very quick steps, and I did
n't see him again till at the supper-table.

At the supper-table he said again, "How do
you do, Mary?" Then he seemed to forget all
about me. At least he did n't say anything more
to me; but three or four times, when I glanced
up, I found him looking at me. But just as soon
as I looked back at him he turned his eyes away
and cleared his throat, and began to eat or to talk
to Aunt Jane.

After dinner — I mean supper — he went out
to the observatory, just as he always used to.
Aunt Jane said her head ached and she was going
to bed. I said I guessed I would step over to Carrie Heywood's; but Aunt Jane said, certainly not;

that I was much too young to be running around
nights in the dark. Nights! And it was only seven
o'clock, and not dark at all! But of course I
could n't go.

Aunt Jane went upstairs, and I was left alone.
I did n't feel a bit like reading; besides, there was
n't a book or a magazine anywhere *asking* you
to read. They just shrieked, "Touch me not!"
behind the glass doors in the library. I hate sewing. I mean *Marie* hates it. Aunt Jane says
Mary's got to learn.

For a time I just walked around the different
rooms downstairs, looking at the chairs and tables and rugs all *just so*, as if they'd been meas-
ured with a yardstick. Marie jerked up a shade
and pushed a chair crooked and kicked a rug
up at one corner; but Mary put them all back
properly — so there was n't any fun in that for
long.

After a while I opened the parlor door and
peeked in. They used to keep it open when
Mother was here; but Aunt Jane does n't use
it. I knew where the electric push button was,
though, and I turned on the light.

It used to be an awful room, and it's worse
now, on account of its shut-up look. Before I got
the light on, the chairs and sofas loomed up like
ghosts in their linen covers. And when the light
did come on, I saw that all the old shiver places

were there. Not one was missing. Great-Grand-
father Anderson's coffin plate on black velvet,
the wax cross and flowers that had been used at
three Anderson funerals, the hair wreath made
of all the hair of seventeen dead Andersons and
five live ones — no, no, I don't mean *all* the hair,
but hair from all seventeen and five. Nurse
Sarah used to tell me about it.

Well, as I said, all the shiver places were there,
and I shivered again as I looked at them; then I
crossed over to Mother's old piano, opened it,
and touched the keys. I love to play. There was
n't any music there, but I don't need music for
lots of my pieces. I know them by heart — only
they're all gay and lively, and twinkly-toe dancy.
Marie music. I don't know a one that would be
proper for *Mary* to play.

But I was just tingling to play *something*, and
I remembered that Father was in the observatory, and Aunt Jane upstairs in the other part of
the house where she could n't possibly hear. So
I began to play. I played the very slowest piece
I had, and I played softly at first; but I know I
forgot, and I know I had n't played two pieces
before I was having the best time ever, and making all the noise I wanted to.

Then all of a sudden I had a funny feeling as
if somebody somewhere was watching me; but
I just could n't turn around. I stopped playing,

though, at the end of that piece, and then I
looked; but there was n't anybody in sight. But
the wax cross was there, and the coffin plate, and
that awful hair wreath; and suddenly I felt as if
that room was just full of folks with great staring
eyes. I fairly shook with shivers then, but I managed to shut the piano and get over to the door
where the light was. Then, a minute later, out
in the big silent hall, I crept on tiptoe toward the
stairs. I knew then, all of a sudden, why I'd felt
somebody was listening. There was. Across the
hall in the library in the big chair before the fire
sat — *Father!* And for 'most a whole half-hour I
had been banging away at that piano on marches
and dance music! My! But I held my breath and
stopped short, I can tell you. But he did n't move
nor turn, and a minute later I was safely by the
door and halfway up the stairs.

I stayed in my room the rest of that evening;
and for the second time since I've been here I
cried myself to sleep.

Another week later.

Well, I've got them — those brown and blue
serge dresses and the calfskin boots. My, but I
hope they're stiff and homely enough — all of
them! And hot, too. Aunt Jane did say to-day
that she did n't know but what she'd made a
mistake not to get gingham dresses. But, then,

she'd have to get the gingham later, anyway, she
said; then I'd have both.

Well, they can't be worse than the serge. That's
sure. I hate the serge. They're awfully homely.
Still, I don't know but it's just as well. Certainly
it's lots easier to be Mary in a brown serge and
clumpy boots than it is in the soft, fluffy things
Marie used to wear. You could n't be Marie in
these things. Honestly, I'm feeling real Maryish
these days.

I wonder if that's why the girls seem so
queer at school. They *are* queer. Three times
lately I've come up to a crowd of girls and
heard them stop talking right off short. They
colored up, too; and pretty quick they began
to slip away, one by one, till there was n't
anybody left but just me, just as they used to
do in Boston. But of course it can't be for the
same reason here, for they've known all along
about the divorce and have n't minded it at
all.

I heard this morning that Stella Mayhew had
a party last night. But *I* did n't get invited. Of
course, you can't always ask everybody to your
parties, but this was a real big party, and I have
n't found a girl in school, yet, that was n't invited — but me. But I guess it was n't anything,
after all. Stella is a new girl that has come here
to live since I went away. Her folks are rich, and

she's very popular, and of course she has loads
of friends she had to invite; and she does n't
know me very well. Probably that was it. And
maybe I just imagine it about the other girls,
too. Perhaps it's the brown serge dress. Still, it
can't be that, for this is the first day I've worn
it. But, as I said, I feel Maryish already.

I have n't dared to touch the piano since that
night a week ago, only once when Aunt Jane was
at a missionary meeting, and I knew Father was
over to the college. But did n't I have a good time
then? I just guess I did!

Aunt Jane does n't care for music. Besides, it's
noisy, she says, and would be likely to disturb
Father. So I'm not to keep on with my music
lessons here. She's going to teach me to sew instead. She says sewing is much more sensible and
useful.

Sensible and useful! I wonder how many times
I've heard those words since I've been here. And
durable, too. And nourishing. That's another
word. Honestly, Marie is getting awfully tired
of Mary's sensible sewing and dusting, and her
durable clumpy shoes and stuffy dresses, and her
nourishing oatmeal and whole-wheat bread. But
there, what can you do? I'm trying to remember
that it's *different*, anyway, and that I said I liked
something different.

I don't see much of Father. Still, there's something kind of queer about it, after all. He only speaks to me about twice a day — just "Good-morning, Mary," and "Good-night." And so far as most of his actions are concerned you would n't think by them that he knew I was in the house. Yet, over and over again at the table, and at times when I did n't even know he was 'round, I've found him watching me, and with such a queer, funny look in his eyes. Then, very quickly always, he looks right away.

But last night he did n't. And that's especially what I wanted to write about to-day. And this is the way it happened.

It was after supper, and I had gone into the library. Father had gone out to the observatory as usual, and Aunt Jane had gone upstairs to her room as usual, and as usual I was wandering 'round looking for something to do. I wanted to play on the piano, but I did n't dare to — not with all those dead-hair and wax-flower folks in the parlor watching me, and the chance of Father's coming in as he did before.

I was standing in the window staring out at nothing — it was n't quite dark yet — when again I had that queer feeling that somebody was looking at me. I turned — and there was Father. He had come in and was sitting in the big chair by the table. But this time he did n't look right away as usual and give me a chance to slip quietly

out of the room, as I always had before. Instead
he said:

"What are you doing there, Mary?"

"N-nothing." I know I stammered. It always
scares me to talk to Father.

"Nonsense!" Father frowned and hitched in
his chair. Father always hitches in his chair when
he's irritated and nervous. "You can't be doing
nothing. Nobody but a dead man does nothing —
and we aren't so sure about him. What are you
doing, Mary?"

"Just l-looking out the window."

"Thank you. That's better. Come here. I want
to talk to you."

"Yes, Father."

I went, of course, at once, and sat down in the
chair near him. He hitched again in his seat.

"Why don't you do something — read, sew,
knit?" he demanded. "Why do I always find you
moping around, doing nothing?"

Just like that he said it; and when he had just
told me —

"Why, Father!" I cried; and I know that I
showed how surprised I was. "I thought you
just said I couldn't do nothing — that nobody
could!"

"Eh? What? Tut, tut!" He seemed very angry at first; then suddenly he looked sharply into
my face. Next, if you'll believe it, he laughed —

the queer little chuckle under his breath that I've heard him give two or three times when there was something he thought was funny. "Humph!" he grunted. Then he gave me another sharp look out of his eyes, and said: "I don't think you meant that to be quite so impertinent as it sounded, Mary, so we'll let it pass — this time. I'll put my question this way: Don't you ever knit or read or sew?"

"I do sew every day in Aunt Jane's room, ten minutes hemming, ten minutes seaming, and ten minutes basting patchwork squares together. I don't know how to knit."

"How about reading? Don't you care for reading?"

"Why, of course I do. I love it!" I cried. "And I do read lots — at home."

"At — *home?*"

I knew then, of course, that I'd made another awful break. There was n't any smile around Father's eyes now, and his lips came together hard and thin over that last word.

"At — at *my* home," I stammered. "I mean, my *other* home."

"Humph!" grunted Father. Then, after a minute: "But why, pray, can't you read here? I'm sure there are — books enough." He flourished his hands toward the bookcases all around the room.

"Oh, I do — a little; but, you see, I'm so afraid I'll leave some of them out when I'm through," I explained.

"Well, what of it? What if you do?" he demanded.

"Why, *Father!*" I tried to show by the way I said it that he knew — of course he knew. But he made me tell him right out that Aunt Jane would n't like it, and that he would n't like it, and that the books always had to be kept exactly where they belonged.

"Well, why not? Why should n't they?" he asked then, almost crossly, and hitching again in his chair. "Are n't books down there — in Boston — kept where they belong, pray?"

It was the first time since I'd come that he'd ever mentioned Boston; and I almost jumped out of my chair when I heard him. But I soon saw it was n't going to be the last, for right then and there he began to question me, even worse than Aunt Jane had.

He wanted to know everything, *everything;* all about the house, with its cushions and cozy corners and curtains 'way up, and books left around easy to get, and magazines, and Baby Lester, and the fun we had romping with him, and everything. Only, of course, I did n't mention Mother. Aunt Jane had told me not to — not anywhere; and to be specially careful before Father. But what can

you do when he asks you himself, right out plain?
And that's what he did.

He'd been up on his feet, tramping up and
down the room all the time I'd been talking; and
now, all of a sudden, he wheels around and stops
short.

"How is — your mother, Mary?" he asks.
And it was just as if he'd opened the door to
another room, he had such a whole lot of questions to ask after that. And when he'd finished he
knew everything: what time we got up and went
to bed, and what we did all day, and the parties
and dinners and auto rides, and the folks that
came such a lot to see Mother.

Then all of a sudden he stopped — asking
questions, I mean. He stopped just as suddenly
as he'd begun. Why, I was right in the middle
of telling about a concert for charity we got up
just before I came away, and how Mother had
practiced for days and days with the young man
who played the violin, when all of a sudden
Father jerked his watch from his pocket and
said:

"There, there, Mary, it's getting late. You've
talked enough — too much. Now go to bed.
Good-night."

Talked too much, indeed! And who'd been
making me do all the talking, I should like to
know? But, of course, I could n't *say* anything.

That's the unfair part of it. Old folks can say anything, *anything* they want to to *you*, but you can't say a thing back to them — not a thing.

And so I went to bed. And the next day all that Father said to me was, "Good-morning, Mary," and, "Good-night," just as he had ever since I came. And that's all he's said yesterday and to-day. But he's looked at me. He's looked at me a lot. I know, because at mealtimes and others, when he's been in the room with me, I've looked up and found his eyes on me. Funny, is n't it?

Two weeks later.

Well, I don't know as I have anything very special to say. Still, I suppose I ought to write something; so I'll put down what little there is.

Of course, there does n't so much happen here, anyway, as there does at home — I mean in Boston. (I *must* stop calling it home down to Boston as if this was n't home at all. It makes Aunt Jane very, very angry, and I don't think Father likes it very well.) But, as I was saying, there really does n't so much happen here as there does down to Boston; and it is n't nearly so interesting. But, there! I suppose I must n't expect it to be interesting. I'm Mary now, not Marie.

There are n't any teas and dinners and pretty ladies and music and soulful-eyed prospective suitors *here*. My! Would n't Aunt Jane have four fits? And Father, too. But I'd just like to put one of Mother's teas with the little cakes and flowers and talk and tinkling laughs down in Aunt Jane's parlor, and then watch what happened. Oh, of course, the party could n't stand it long — not in there with the hair wreath and the coffin plate. But they could stand it long enough for Father to thunder from the library, "Jane, what in Heaven's name is the meaning of all this?" And for Aunt Jane to give one look at the kind of clothes *real* folks wear, and then flee with her hands to her ears and her eyes upraised to the ceiling. Would n't it be fun?

But, there! What's the use of imagining perfectly crazy, impossible things like that? We have n't had a thing here in that parlor since I came but one missionary meeting and one Ladies' Aid Sewing Circle; and after the last one (the Sewing Circle) Aunt Jane worked a whole day picking threads off the carpet, and smoothing down the linen covers because they'd got so mussed up. And I heard her tell the hired girl that she should n't have that Sewing Circle here again in a hurry, and when she did have them they'd have to sew in the dining-room with a sheet spread down to catch the threads. My! but I would like to see Aunt Jane with one of Mother's teas in her parlor!

I can't see as Father has changed much of any

these last two weeks. He still does n't pay much
of any attention to me, though I do find him
looking at me sometimes, just as if he was trying to make up his mind about something. He
does n't say hardly anything to me, only once or
twice when he got to asking questions again
about Boston and Mother.

The last time I told him all about Mr. Harlow,
and he was so interested! I just happened to mention his name, and he wanted to know right away
if it was Mr. Carl Harlow, and if I knew whether
Mother had ever known him before. And of
course I told him right away that it was — the
same one she was engaged to before she was engaged to him.

Father looked funny and kind of grunted and
said, yes, yes, he knew. Then he said, "That will
do, Mary." And he began to read his book again.
But he never turned a page, and it was n't five
minutes before he got up and walked around the
room, picking out books from the bookcases and
putting them right back, and picking up things
from the mantel and putting *them* right back.
Then he turned to me and asked with a kind of
of-course-I-don't-care air:

"Did you say you saw quite a little of — this
Harlow fellow?"

But he did care. I know he did. He was *real* interested. I could see that he was. And so I told

him everything, all about how he came there to the teas, and sent her flowers and candy, and was getting a divorce himself, and what he said on the sofa that day, and how Mother answered. As I said, I told him everything, only I was careful not to call Mr. Harlow a prospective suitor, of course. I remembered too well what Aunt Hattie had said. Father did n't say anything when I got through. He just got up and left the room, and pretty quick I saw him crossing the lawn to the observatory.

I guess there are n't any prospective suitors here. I mean, I guess Father is n't a prospective suitor — anyhow, not yet. (Of course, it 's the man that has to be the suitor.) He does n't go anywhere, only over to the college and out to the observatory. I 've watched so to see. I wanted specially to know, for of course if he was being a prospective suitor to any one, she 'd be my new mother, maybe. And I 'm going to be awfully particular about any new mother coming into the house.

A whole lot more, even, depends on mothers than on fathers, you know; and if you 're going to have one all ready-made thrust upon you, you are sort of anxious to know what kind she is. Some way, I don't think I 'd like a new mother even as well as I 'd like a new father; and I don't believe I 'd like *him* very well.

Of course, there are quite a lot of ladies here that Father *could* have. There are several pretty teachers in the schools, and some nice unmarried ladies in the church. And there's Miss Parmelia Snow. She's Professor Snow's sister. She wears glasses and is terribly learned. Maybe he *would* like her. But, mercy! I should n't.

Then there's Miss Grace Ann Sanborn. She's fat, and awfully jolly. She comes here a lot lately to see Aunt Jane. I don't know why. They don't belong to the same church, or anything. But she "runs over," as she calls it, almost every afternoon just a little before dinner — I mean supper.

Mrs. Darling used to come then, too, when I first came; but she comes over evenings now more. Maybe it's because she does n't like Miss Grace Ann. I don't think she *does* like her, for every time she saw her, she'd say: "Oh, *you?* So you're here!" And then she'd turn and talk to Aunt Jane and simply ignore Miss Grace Ann. And pretty quick she'd get up and go. And now she comes evenings. She's fixing over her house, and she runs and asks Aunt Jane's advice about every little thing. She asks Father's, too, every chance she gets, when she sees him in the hall or on the front steps. I heard her tell Aunt Jane she considered Professor Anderson a man of most excellent taste and judgment.

I suppose Mrs. Darling *could* be my new

mother. She's a widow. Her husband died last year. She is very well off now that her husband is dead, I heard Aunt Jane say one day. She meant well off in money — quite a lot of it, you know. I *thought* she meant well off because he was dead and she did n't have to live with him any more, and I said so to Aunt Jane. (He was a cross man, and very stern, as everybody knew.) But, dear suz me! Aunt Jane was awfully shocked, and said certainly not; that she meant Mr. Darling had left his wife a great deal of money.

Then she talked very stern and solemn to me, and said that I must not think just because my poor dear father's married life had ended in such a wretched tragedy that every other home had such a skeleton in the closet.

I grew stern and dignified and solemn then. I knew, of course, what she meant. I'm no child. She meant Mother. She meant that Mother, my dear blessed mother, was the skeleton in their closet. And of course I was n't going to stand there and hear that, and not say a word.

But I did n't say just a word. I said a good many words. I won't try to put them all down here; but I told her quietly, in a firm voice, and with no temper (showing), that I guessed Father was just as much of a skeleton in Mother's closet as she was in his; and that if she could see how perfectly happy my mother was now she'd understand a little of what my father's skeleton had done to her all those years she'd had to live with it.

I said a lot more, but before I'd got half finished with what I wanted to say, I got to crying, so I just had to run out of the room.

That night I heard Aunt Jane tell Mrs. Darling that the worst feature of the whole deplorable situation was the effect on the child's mind, and the wretched conception it gave her of the sacredness of the marriage tie, or something like that. And Mrs. Darling sighed, and said, oh, and ah, and the pity of it.

I don't like Mrs. Darling.

Of course, as I said before, Mrs. Darling could be my new mother, being a widow, so. But, mercy! I hope she won't. I'd rather have Miss Grace Ann than her, and I should n't be crazy about having Miss Grace Ann.

Well, I guess there's nothing more to write. Things at school are just the same, only more so. The girls are getting so they act almost as bad as those down to Boston in the school where I went before I changed. Of course, maybe it's the divorce here, same as it was there. But I don't see how it can be that here. Why, they've known it from the very first!

Oh, dear suz me! How I do wish I could see Mother to-night and have her take me in her

arms and kiss me. I'm so tired of being Mary
'way off up here where nobody cares or wants me.

Even Father does n't want me, not really want
me. I know he does n't. I don't see why he keeps
me, only I suppose he'd be ashamed not to take
me his six months as long as the court gave me to
him for that time.

Another two weeks later.

I'm so angry I can hardly write, and at the
same time I'm so angry I've just got to write. I
can't talk. There is n't anybody to talk to; and
I've got to tell somebody. So I'm going to tell it
here.

I've found out now what's the matter with the
girls — you know I said there *was* something the
matter with them; that they acted queer and
stopped talking when I came up, and faded away
till there was n't anybody but me left; and about
the party Stella Mayhew had and did n't invite
me.

Well, it's been getting worse and worse. Other
girls have had parties, and more and more often
the girls have stopped talking and have looked
queer when I came up. We got up a secret society
and called it the "Tony Ten," and I was going to
be its president. Then all of a sudden one day I
found there was n't any Tony Ten — only Carrie
Heywood and me. The other eight had formed

another society and Stella Mayhew was their
president.

I told Carrie we would n't care; that we'd just
change it and call it the "Tony Two"; and that
two was a lot more exclusive than ten, anyway.
But I did care, and Carrie did. I knew she did.
And I know it better now because last night —
she told me. You see things have been getting
simply unbearable these last few days, and it got
so it looked as if I was n't even going to have
Carrie left. *She* began to act queer and I accused
her of it, and told her if she did n't want to belong
to the Tony Two she need n't. That I did n't
care; that I'd be a secret society all by myself.
But I cried. I could n't help crying; and she knew
I did — care. Then she began to cry; and to-day,
after school, we went to walk up on the hill to the
big rock; and there — she told me. And it *was*
the divorce.

And it's all that Stella Mayhew — the new
girl. Her mother found out I was divorced (I
mean Mother was) and she told Stella not to play
with me, nor speak to me, nor have a thing to do
with me. And I said to Carrie, all right! Who
cared? *I* did n't. That I never had liked that
Mayhew girl, anyway. But Carrie said that
was n't all. She said Stella had got to be real popular before I came; that her folks had lots of
money, and she always had candy and could

treat to ice-cream and auto rides, and everybody
with her was sure of a good time. She had parties,
too — lots of them; and of course, all the girls
and boys liked that.

Well, when I came everything was all right till
Stella's mother found out about the divorce, and
then — well, then things were different. First Stella
contented herself with making fun of me, Carrie
said. She laughed at the serge dresses and big
homely shoes, and then she began on my name,
and said the idea of being called Mary by Father
and Marie by Mother, and that 't was just like
Dr. Jekyll and Mr. Hyde. (That's a story, Carrie
says. I'm going to read it, if Father's got it. If
there ever was another Mary and Marie all in one
in the world I want to know what she did.) But
Carrie says the poking fun at me did n't make
much difference with the girls, so Stella tried
something else. She not only would n't speak to
me herself, or invite me, or anything, but she
told all the girls that they could n't go with her
and me, too. That they might take their choice.
And Carrie said some of them did choose and
stayed with me; but they lost all the good times
and ice-cream and parties and rides and everything; and so one by one they dropped me and
went back to Stella, and now there was n't anybody left, only her, Carrie. And then she began
to cry.

And when she stopped speaking, and I knew all, and saw her crying there before me, and thought of my dear blessed mother, I was so angry I could scarcely speak. I just shook with righteous indignation. And in my most superb, haughty, and disdainful manner I told Carrie Heywood to dry her tears; that she need n't trouble herself any further, nor worry about losing any more ice-cream nor parties. That I would hereto declare our friendship null and void, and this day set my hand and seal to never speak to her again, if she liked, and considered that necessary to keeping the acquaintance of the precious Stella.

But she cried all the more at that, and flung herself upon me, and, of course, I began to cry, too — and you can't stay superb and haughty and disdainful when you 're all the time trying to hunt up a handkerchief to wipe away the tears that are coursing down your wan cheeks. And of course I did n't. We had a real good cry together, and vowed we loved each other better than ever, and nobody could come between us, not even bringing a chocolate-fudge-marshmallow college ice — which we both adore. But I told her that she would be all right, just the same, for of course I should never step my foot inside of that school-house again. That I could n't, out of respect to Mother. That I should tell Aunt Jane that to-

morrow morning. There is n't any other school
here, so they can't send me anywhere else. But
it's 'most time for school to close, anyway. There
are only two weeks more.

But I don't think that will make any difference
to Aunt Jane. It's the principle of the thing. It's
always the principle of the thing with Aunt Jane.
She'll be very angry, I know. Maybe she'll send
me home. Oh, I *hope* she will!

Well, I shall tell her to-morrow, anyway. Then
— we'll see.

One day later.

And, dear, dear, what a day it has been!

I told her this morning. She was very angry.
She said at first: "Nonsense, Mary, don't be impertinent. Of course you'll go to school!" and all
that kind of talk. But I kept my temper. I did not
act angry. I was simply firm and dignified. And
when she saw I really meant what I said, and that
I would not step my foot inside that schoolroom
again — that it was a matter of conscience with
me — that I did not think it was *right* for me to
do it, she simply stared for a minute, as if she
could n't believe her eyes and ears. Then she
gasped:

"Mary, what do you mean by such talk to me?
Do you think I shall permit this sort of thing to
go on for a moment?"

I thought then she was going to send me home. Oh, I did so hope she was. But she did n't. She sent me to my room.

"You will stay there until your father comes home this noon," she said. "This is a matter for him to settle."

Father! And I never even thought of her going to *him* with it. She was always telling me never to bother Father with anything, and I knew she did n't usually ask him anything about me. She settled everything herself. But *this* — and the very thing I did n't want her to ask him, too. But of course I could n't help myself. That's the trouble. Youth is *so* helpless in the clutches of old age!

Well, I went to my room. Aunt Jane told me to meditate on my sins. But I did n't. I meditated on other people's sins. *I* did n't have any to meditate on. Was it a sin, pray, for me to stand up for my mother and refuse to associate with people who would n't associate with *me* on account of *her?* I guess not!

I meditated on Stella Mayhew and her mother, and on those silly, faithless girls that thought more of an ice-cream soda than they did of justice and right to their fellow schoolmate. And I meditated on Aunt Jane and her never giving me so much as a single kiss since I came. And I meditated on how much better Father liked stars and

comets than he did his own daughter; and I meditated on what a cruel, heartless world this is,
anyway, and what a pity it was that I, so fair and
young, should have found it out so soon — right
on the bank, as it were, or where that brook and
river meet. And I wondered, if I died if anybody
would care; and I thought how beautiful and
pathetic I would look in my coffin with my lily-
white hands folded on my breast. And I *hoped*
they'd have the funeral in the daytime, because if
it was at night-time Father'd be sure to have a
star or something to keep *him* from coming. And
I *wanted* him to come. I *wanted* him to feel bad;
and I meditated on how bad he would feel —
when it was too late.

But even with all this to meditate on, it was an
awfully long time coming noon; and they did n't
call me down to dinner even then. Aunt Jane sent
up two pieces of bread without any butter and a
glass of water. How like Aunt Jane — making
even my dinner a sin to meditate on! Only she
would call it *my* sin, and I would call it hers.

Well, after dinner Father sent for me to come
down to the library. So I knew then, of course,
that Aunt Jane had told him. I did n't know but
she would wait until night. Father usually spends
his hour after dinner reading in the library and
must n't be disturbed. But evidently to-day Aunt
Jane thought I was more consequence than his

reading. Anyhow, she told him, and he sent for
me.

My, but I hated to go! Fathers and Aunt Janes
are two different propositions. Fathers have more
rights and privileges, of course. Everybody knows
that.

Well, I went into the library. Father stood with
his back to the fireplace and his hands in his
pockets. He was plainly angry at being disturbed.
Anybody could see that. He began speaking at
once, the minute I got into the room — very
cold and dignified.

"Mary, your aunt tells me you have been disobedient and disrespectful to her. Have you anything to say?"

I shook my head and said, "No, sir."

What could I say? Old folks ask such senseless
questions, sometimes. Naturally I wasn't going
to say I *had* been disrespectful and disobedient
when I had n't; and of course, I could n't say I
had n't been when Aunt Jane said I *had*. That
would be just like saying Aunt Jane lied. So, of
course, I had nothing to say. And I said so.

"But she declares you refused to go back to
school, Mary," said Father then.

"Yes, sir."

"Then you did refuse?"

"Yes, sir."

"Well, you may go and tell her now, please,

that you are sorry, and that you will go to school
this afternoon. You may go now." And he turned
to the table and picked up his book.

I did n't go, of course. I just stood there
twisting my handkerchief in my fingers; and, of
course, right away he saw me. He had sat down
then.

"Mary, did n't you hear me?" he demanded.

"Yes, sir, but — Father, I *can't* go back to
that school," I choked. And I began to cry.

"But I tell you that you must."

I shook my head.

"I can't."

"Do you mean that you defy me as you did
your Aunt Jane this morning? — that you refuse
to go back to school?"

"Yes, sir."

For a minute he sat and stared at me just as
Aunt Jane had done; then he lifted his head and
threw back his shoulders as if he was throwing
off a heavy weight.

"Come, come, Mary," he said sternly. "I am
not a patient man, and my temper has reached
the breaking point. You will go back to school
and you will go now. I mean that, Mary."

"But, Father, I *can't*," I choked again; and I
guess there was something in my face this time
that made even him see. For again he just stared
for a minute, and then said:

"Mary, what in the world does this mean? Why can't you go back? Have you been — expelled?"

"Oh, no, sir."

"Then you mean you won't go back."

"I mean I *can't* — on account of Mother."

I would n't have said it if I had n't had to. I did n't want to tell him, but I knew from the very first that I'd have to tell him before I got through. I could see it in his face. And so, now, with his eyes blazing as he jumped almost out of his chair and exclaimed, "Your mother!" I let it out and got it over as soon as possible.

"I mean, on account of Mother — that not for you, or Aunt Jane, or anybody will I go back to that school and associate with folks that won't associate with me — on account of Mother."

And then I told it — all about the girls, Stella Mayhew, Carrie, and how they acted, and what they said about my being Dr. Jekyll and Mr. Hyde because I was a Mary and a Marie, and the ice-cream, and the parties they had to give up if they went with *me*. And I know I was crying so I could hardly speak before I finished; and Father was on his feet tramping up and down the room muttering something under his breath, and looking — oh, I can't begin to tell how he looked. But it was awful.

"And so that's why I wish," I finished chokingly, "that it would hurry up and be a year, so Mother could get married."

"*Married!*" Like a flash he turned and stopped short, staring at me.

"Why, yes," I explained; "for if she *did* get married, she would n't be divorced any longer, would she?"

But he would n't answer. With a queer little noise in his throat he turned again and began to walk up and down, up and down, until I thought for a minute he'd forgotten I was there. But he had n't. For after a while he stopped again right in front of me.

"So your mother is thinking of getting married," he said in a voice so queer it sounded as if it had come from away off somewhere.

But I shook my head and said no, of course; and that I was very sure she would n't till her year was up, and even then I did n't know which she'd take, so I could n't tell for sure anything about it. But I hoped she'd take one of them, so she would n't be divorced any longer.

"But you don't know *which* she'll take," grunted Father again. He turned then, and began to walk up and down again, with his hands in his pockets; and I did n't know whether to go away or to stay, and I suppose I'd have been there now if Aunt Jane had n't suddenly appeared in the library doorway.

"Charles, if Mary is going to school at all to-day it is high time she was starting," she said. But Father did n't seem to hear. He was still tramping up and down the room, his hands in his pockets.

"Charles!" Aunt Jane raised her voice and spoke again. "I said if Mary is going to school at all to-day it is high time she was starting."

"Eh? What?" If you'll believe it, that man looked as dazed as if he'd never even *heard* of my going to school. Then suddenly his face changed. "Oh, yes, to be sure. Well, er — Mary is not going to school to-day," he said. Then he looked at his watch, and without another word strode into the hall, got his hat, and left the house, leaving Aunt Jane and me staring into each other's faces.

But I did n't stay much longer than Father did. I strode into the hall, too, by Aunt Jane. But I did n't leave the house. I came up here to my own room; and ever since I've been writing it all down in my book.

Of course, I don't know now what's going to happen next. But I *wish* you could have seen Aunt Jane's face when Father said I was n't going to school to-day! I don't believe she's sure yet that she heard aright — though she did n't try to stop me, or even speak when I left and came up-stairs. But I just know she's keeping up a power-ful thinking.

For that matter, so am I. What *is* going to happen next? Have I got to go to school to-morrow? But then, of course, I shan't do that. Besides, I don't believe Father 'll ask me to, after what I said about Mother. *He* did n't like that — what those girls said — any better than I did. I 'm sure of that. Why, he looked simply furious. But there is n't any other school here that I can be sent to, and —

But what 's the use? I might surmise and speculate all day and not come anywhere near the truth. I must await — what the night will bring forth, as they say in really truly novels.

Four days later.

And what did the night bring forth? Yes, what did it bring! Verily it brought forth one thing I thought nothing ever could have brought forth.

It was like this.

That night at the supper-table Aunt Jane cleared her throat in the I-am-determined-I-will-speak kind of a way that she always uses when she speaks to Father. (Aunt Jane does n't talk to Father much more than Mother used to.)

"Charles," she began.

Father had an astronomy paper beside his plate, and he was so busy reading he did n't hear, so Aunt Jane had to speak again — a little louder this time.

"Charles, I have something to say to you."

"Eh? What? Oh — er — yes. Well, Jane, what is it?" Father was looking up with his I'll-be-patient-if-it-kills-me air, and with his forefinger down on his paper to keep his place.

As if anybody could talk to a person who's simply tolerating you for a minute like that, with his forefinger holding on to what he *wants* to tend to! Why, I actually found myself being sorry for Aunt Jane.

She cleared her throat again.

"It is understood, of course, that Mary is to go to school to-morrow morning, I suppose," she said.

"Why, of course, of course," began Father impatiently, looking down at his paper. "Of course she'll go to —" he stopped suddenly. A complete change came to his face. He grew red, then white. His eyes sort of flashed. "School?" he said then, in a hard, decided voice. "Oh, no; Mary is not going to school to-morrow morning." He looked down to his paper and began to read again. For him the subject was very evidently closed. But for Aunt Jane it was *not* closed.

"You don't mean, Charles, that she is not to go to school at all, any more," she gasped.

"Exactly." Father read on in his paper without looking up.

"But, Charles, to stop her school like this!"

"Why not? It closes in a week or two, any-way."

Aunt Jane's lips came together hard.

"That's not the question at all," she said, cold like ice. "Charles, I'm amazed at you — yielding to that child's whims like this — that she does n't want to go to school! It's the principle of the thing that I'm objecting to. Do you realize what it will lead to — what it —"

"Jane!" With a jerk Father sat up straight. "I realize some things that perhaps you do not. But that is neither here nor there. I do not wish Mary to go to school any more this spring. That is all; and I think — it is sufficient."

"Certainly." Aunt Jane's lips came together again grim and hard. "Perhaps you will be good enough to say what she *shall* do with her time."

"Time? Do? Why — er — what she always does; read, sew, study —"

"Study?" Aunt Jane asked the question with a hateful little smile that Father would have been blind not to have understood. And he was equal to it — but I 'most fell over backward when I found *how* equal to it he was.

"Certainly," he says, "study. I — I'll hear her lessons myself — in the library, after I come home in the afternoon. Now let us hear no more about it."

With that he pushed back his plate, stuffed

his astronomy paper into his pocket, and left the
table, without waiting for dessert. And Aunt
Jane and I were left alone.

I did n't say anything. Victors should n't
boast — and I was a victor, of course, about the
school. But when I thought of what Father had
said about my reciting my lessons to him every
day in the library — I was n't so sure whether
I'd won out or not. Recite lessons to my father?
Why, I could n't even imagine such a thing!

Aunt Jane did n't say anything either. I guess
she did n't know what to say. And it was kind
of a queer situation, when you came right down
to it. Both of us sitting there and knowing
I was n't going back to school any more, and I
knowing why, and knowing Aunt Jane did n't
know why. (Of course I had n't told Aunt Jane
about Mother and Mrs. Mayhew.) It would be a
funny world, would n't it, if we all knew what
each other was thinking all the time? Why, we'd
get so we would n't do anything *but* think — for
there would n't any of us *speak* to each other, I'm
afraid, we'd be so angry at what the other was
thinking.

Well, Aunt Jane and I did n't speak that night
at the supper-table. We finished in stern silence;
then Aunt Jane went upstairs to her room and
I went up to mine. (You see what a perfectly
wildly exciting life Mary is living! And when

I think of how *full* of good times Mother wanted every minute to be. But that was for Marie, of course.)

The next morning after breakfast Aunt Jane said:

"You will spend your forenoon studying, Mary. See that you learn well your lessons, so as not to annoy your father."

"Yes, Aunt Jane," said Mary, polite and proper, and went upstairs obediently; but even Mary did n't know exactly how to study those lessons.

Carrie had brought me all my books from school. I had asked her to when I knew that I was not going back. There were the lessons that had been assigned for the next day, of course, and I supposed probably Father would want me to study those. But I could n't imagine Father teaching *me* all alone. And how was I ever going to ask him questions, if there were things I did n't understand? Besides, I could n't imagine myself reciting lessons to Father — *Father!*

But I need n't have worried. If I could only have known. Little did I think — But, there, this is no way to tell a story. I read in a book, "How to Write a Novel," that you must n't "anticipate." (*I* thought folks always anticipated novels. I do. I thought you wanted them to.)

Well, to go on.

Father got home at four o'clock. I saw him come up the walk, and I waited till I was sure he'd got settled in the library, then I went down.

He was n't there.

A minute later I saw him crossing the lawn to the observatory. Well, what to do I did n't know. Mary said to go after him; but Marie said nay, nay. And in spite of being Mary just now, I let Marie have her way.

Rush after him and tell him he'd forgotten to hear my lessons? *Father?* Well, I guess not! Besides, it was n't my fault. *I* was there all ready. It was n't my blame that he was n't there to hear me. But he might remember and come back. Well, if he did, *I'd* be there. So I went to one of those bookcases and pulled out a touch-me-not book from behind the glass door. Then I sat down and read till the supper-bell rang.

Father was five minutes late to supper. I don't know whether he looked at me or not. I did n't dare to look at him — until Aunt Jane said, in her chilliest manner:

"I trust your daughter had good lessons, Charles."

I *had* to look at him then. I just could n't look anywhere else. So I was looking straight at him when he gave that funny little startled glance into my eyes. And into his eyes then there crept the funniest, dearest little understanding twinkle

— and I suddenly realized that Father, *Father*, was laughing with me at a little secret between *us*. But 't was only for a second. The next moment his eyes were very grave and looking at Aunt Jane.

"I have no cause to complain — of my daughter's lessons to-day," he said very quietly. Then he glanced over at me again. But I had to look away *quick*, or I would have laughed right out.

When he got up from the table he said to me: "I shall expect to see you to-morrow in the library at four, Mary."

And Mary answered, "Yes, Father," polite and proper, as she should; but Marie inside was just chuckling with the joke of it all.

The next day I watched again at four for Father to come up the walk; and when he had come in I went down to the library. He was there in his pet seat before the fireplace. (Father always sits before the fireplace, whether there's a fire there or not. And sometimes he looks *so* funny sitting there, staring into those gray ashes just as if it was the liveliest kind of a fire he was watching.)

As I said, he was there, but I had to speak twice before he looked up. Then, for a minute, he stared vaguely.

"Eh? Oh! Ah — er — yes, to be sure," he muttered then. "You have come with your books. Yes, I remember."

But there was n't any twinkle in his eyes, nor the least little bit of an understanding smile; and I *was* disappointed. I *had* been looking for it. I knew then, when I felt so suddenly lost and heart-achey, that I had been expecting and planning all day on that twinkly understanding smile. You know you feel worse when you've just found a father and then lost him!

And I had lost him. I knew it the minute he sighed and frowned and got up from his seat and said, oh, yes, to be sure. He was just Dr. Anderson then — the man who knew all about the stars, and who had been unmarried to Mother, and who called me "Mary" in an of-course-you're-my-daughter tone of voice.

Well, he took my books and heard my lessons, and told me what I was to study next day. He's done that two days now.

Oh, I'm so tired of being Mary! And I've got more than four whole months of it left. I did n't get Mother's letter to-day. Maybe that's why I'm specially lonesome to-night.

July first.

School is done, both the regular school and my school. Not that my school has amounted to much. Really it has n't. Oh, for three or four days he asked questions quite like just a teacher. Then he got to talking. Sometimes it would be about something in the lessons; sometimes it would be about a star, or the moon. And he'd get so interested that I'd think for a minute that maybe the understanding twinkle would come into his eyes again. But it never did.

Sometimes it wasn't stars and moons, though, that he talked about. It was Boston, and Mother. Yes, he did. He talked a lot about Mother. As I look back at it now, I can see that he did. He asked me all over again what she did, and about the parties, and the folks that came to see her. He asked again about Mr. Harlow, and about the concert, and the young man who played the violin, and what was his name, and how old was he, and did I like him. And then, right in the middle of some question, or rather, right in the middle of some *answer* I was giving *him*, he would suddenly remember he was hearing my lessons, and he would say, "Come, come, Mary, what has this to do with your lessons?"

Just as if I was to blame! (But, then, we women always get the blame, I notice.) And then he'd attend strictly to the books for maybe five whole minutes — before he asked another question about that party, or the violinist.

Naturally the lessons haven't amounted to much, as you can imagine. But the term was nearly finished, anyway; and my *real* school is in Boston, of course.

It's vacation now. I do hope *that* will amount to something!

August first.

It hasn't, so far — I mean vacation. Really, what a world of disappointment this is! How on earth I'm going to stand being Mary for three months more I don't know. But I've got to, I suppose. I've been here May, June, and July; and that leaves August, September, and October yet to come. And when I think of Mother and Boston and Marie, and the darling good times down there where you're really *wanted*, I am simply crazy.

If Father wanted me, really wanted me, I would n't care a bit. I'd be willing to be Mary six whole months. Yes, I'd be *glad* to. But he does n't. I'm just here by order of the court. And what can you do when you're nothing but a daughter by order of the court?

Since the lessons have stopped, Father's gone back to his "Good-morning, Mary," and "Good-night," and nothing else, day in and day out. Lately he's got so he hangs around the house an awful lot, too, so I can't even do the things I did the first of the month. I mean that I'd been playing some on the piano, along at the first, after school closed. Aunt Jane was out in the garden a lot, and Father out to the observatory, so I just reveled in piano-playing till I found almost every time I did it that he had come back, and was in the library with the door open. So I don't dare to play now.

And there is n't a blessed thing to do. Oh, I have to sew an hour, and now I have to weed an hour, too; and Aunt Jane tried to have me learn to cook; but Susie (in the kitchen) flatly refused to have me "messing around," so Aunt Jane had to give that up. Susie's the one person Aunt Jane's afraid of, you see. She always threatens to leave if anything goes across her wishes. So Aunt Jane has to be careful. I heard her tell Mrs. Small next door that good hired girls were awfully scarce in Andersonville.

As I said before, if only there was somebody here that wanted me. But there is n't. Of course Father does n't. That goes without saying. And Aunt Jane does n't. That goes, too, without saying. Carrie Heywood has gone away for all summer, so I can't have even her; and of course, I would n't associate with any of the other girls, even if they would associate with me — which they won't.

That leaves only Mother's letters. They are dear, and I love them. I don't know what I'd do without them. And yet, sometimes I think

maybe they're worse than if I did n't have them.
They make me so homesick, and I always cry so
after I get them. Still, I know I just could n't
live a minute if 't was n't for Mother's letters.

Besides being so lonesome there's another
thing that worries me, too; and that is, *this* —
what I'm writing, I mean. The novel. It's getting
awfully stupid. Nothing happens. *Nothing!* Of
course, if 't was just a story I could make up
things — lots of them — exciting, interesting
things, like having Mother elope with the violinist, and Father shoot him and fall in love with
Mother all over again, or else with somebody
else, and shoot that one's lover. Or maybe somebody'd try to shoot Father, and I'd get there
just in time to save him. Oh, I'd *love* that!

But this is a real story, so, of course, I can't
put in anything only just what happens; and
nothing happens.

And that's another thing. About the love story
— I'm afraid there is n't going to be one. Anyway, there is n't a bit of a sign of one, yet, unless
it's Mother. And of course, I have n't seen her
for three months, so I can't say anything about
that.

Father has n't got one. I'm sure of that. He
does n't like ladies. I know he does n't. He always
runs away from them. But they don't run away
from him! Listen.

As I said before, quite a lot of them call here to see Aunt Jane, and they come lots of times evenings and late afternoons, and I know now why they do it. They come then because they think Father'll be at home at that time; and they want to see him.

I know it now, but I never thought of it till the other day when I heard our hired girl, Susie, talking about it with Bridget, the Smalls' hired girl, over the fence when I was weeding the garden one day. Then I knew. It was like this:

Mrs. Darling had been over the night before as usual, and had stayed an awfully long time talking to Aunt Jane on the front piazza. Father had been there, too, awhile. She stopped him on his way into the house. I was there and I heard her. She said:

"Oh, Mr. Anderson, I'm so glad I saw you! I wanted to ask your advice about selling poor dear Mr. Darling's law library."

And then she went on to tell him how she'd had an offer, but she wasn't sure whether it was a good one or not. And she told him how highly she prized his opinion, and he was a man of such splendid judgment, and she felt so alone now with no strong man's shoulder to lean upon, and she would be so much obliged if he only would tell her whether he considered that offer a good one or not.

Father hitched and ahemmed and moved

nearer the door all the time she was talking, and he did n't seem to hear her when she pushed a chair toward him and asked him to please sit down and tell her what to do; that she was so alone in the world since poor dear Mr. Darling had gone. (She always calls him poor dear Mr. Darling now, but Susie says she did n't when he was alive; she called him something quite different. I wonder what it was.)

Well, as I said, Father hitched and fidgeted, and said he did n't know, he was sure; that she'd better take wiser counsel than his, and that he was very sorry, but she really must excuse him. And he got through the door while he was talking just as fast as he could himself, so that she could n't get in a single word to keep him. Then he was gone.

Mrs. Darling stayed on the piazza two whole hours longer, but Father never came out at all again.

It was the next morning that Susie said this over the back-yard fence to Bridget:

"It does beat all how popular this house is with the ladies — after college hours!"

And Bridget chuckled and answered back:

"Sure it is! An' I do be thinkin' the Widder Darlin' is a heap fonder of Miss Jane now than she would have been had poor dear Mr. Darlin' lived!"

And she chuckled again, and so did Susie. And then, all of a sudden, I knew. It was Father all those ladies wanted. It was Father Mrs. Darling wanted. They came here to see him. They wanted to marry him. *They* were the prospective suitors. As if I did n't know what Susie and Bridget meant! I'm no child!

But all this does n't make Father like *them*. I'm not sure but it makes him dislike them. Anyhow, he won't have anything to do with them. He always runs away over to the observatory, or somewhere, and won't see them; and I've heard him say things about them to Aunt Jane, too — words that sound all right, but that don't mean what they say, and everybody knows they don't. So, as I said before, I don't see any chance of Father's having a love story to help out this book — not right away, anyhow.

As for *my* love story — I don't see any chance of that's beginning, either. Yet, seems as if there ought to be the beginning of it by this time — I'm going on fifteen. Oh, there have been *beginnings*, lots of them — only Aunt Jane would n't let them go on and be endings, though I told her good and plain that I thought it perfectly all right; and I reminded her about the brook and river meeting where I stood, and all that.

But I could n't make her see it at all. She said, "Stuff and nonsense" — and when Aunt Jane says *both* stuff and nonsense I know there's nothing *doing*. (Oh, dear, that's slang! Aunt Jane says she does wish I would eliminate the slang from my vocabulary. Well, I wish *she'd* climinate some of the long words from *hers*. Marie said that — not Mary.)

Well, Aunt Jane said stuff and nonsense, and that I was much too young to run around with silly boys. You see, Charlie Smith had walked home from school with me twice, but I had to stop that. And Fred Small was getting so he was over here a lot. Aunt Jane stopped *him*. Paul Mayhew — yes, *Paul Mayhew*, Stella's brother! — came home with me, too, and asked me to go with him auto-riding. My, how I did want to go! I wanted the ride, of course, but especially I wanted to go because he was Mrs. Mayhew's son. I just wanted to show Mrs. Mayhew! But Aunt Jane wouldn't let me. That's the time she talked specially about running around with silly boys. But she need n't have. Paul is no silly boy. He's old enough to get a license to drive his own car.

But it was n't just because he was young that Aunt Jane refused. I found out afterward. It was because he was any kind of a man paying me attention. I found that out through Mr. Claude Livingstone. Mr. Livingstone brings our groceries. He's a *real* young gentleman — tall, black mustache, and lovely dark eyes. He goes to our church, and he asked me to go to the Sunday-School picnic with him. I was *so* pleased. And I supposed, of course, Aunt Jane would let me go with *him*. *He's* no silly boy! Besides, I knew him real well, and liked him. I used to talk to him quite a lot when he brought the groceries.

But did Aunt Jane let me go? She did not. Why, she seemed almost more shocked than she had been over Charlie Smith and Fred Small, and the others.

"Mercy, child!" she exclaimed. "Where in the world do you pick up these people?" And she brought out that "these people" *so* disagreeably! Why, you'd think Mr. Livingstone was a foreign Japanese, or something.

I told her then quietly, and with dignity, and with no temper (showing), that Mr. Livingstone was not a foreign Japanese, but was a very nice gentleman; and that I had not picked him up. He came to her own door himself, almost every day.

"My own door!" exclaimed Aunt Jane. And she looked absolutely frightened. "You mean to tell me that that creature has been coming here to see you, and I not know it?"

I told her then — again quietly and with dignity, and without temper (showing) — that he had been coming, not to see me, but in the natural pursuance of his profession of delivering groceries. And I said that he was not a creature. On the contrary, he was, I was sure, an estimable young man. He went to her own church and Sunday-School. Besides, I could vouch for him myself, as I knew him well, having seen and talked with him almost every day for a long while, when he came to the house.

But nothing I could say seemed to have the least effect upon her at all, only to make her angrier and angrier, if anything. In fact *I* think she showed a great deal of temper for a Christian woman about a fellow Christian in her own church.

But she would n't let me go to the picnic; and not only that, but I think she changed grocers, for Mr. Livingstone has n't been here for a long time, and when I asked Susie where he was she looked funny, and said we were n't getting our groceries where Mr. Livingstone worked any longer.

Well, of course, that ended that. And there has n't been any other since. That 's why I say *my* love story does n't seem to be getting along very well. Naturally, when it gets noised around town that your Aunt Jane won't let you go anywhere with a young man, or let a young man come to see you, or even walk home with you after the first time — why, the young men are n't going to do very much toward making your daily life into a love story.

Two weeks later.

A queer thing happened last night. It was like this:

I think I said before what an awfully stupid time Mary is having of it, and how I could n't play now, or make any noise, 'cause Father has taken to hanging around the house so much. Well, listen what happened.

Yesterday Aunt Jane went to spend the day with her best friend. She said for me not to leave the house, as some member of the family should be there. She told me to sew an hour, weed an hour, dust the house downstairs and upstairs, and read some improving book an hour. The rest of the time I might amuse myself.

Amuse myself! A jolly time I could have all by myself! Even Father was n't to be home for dinner, so I would n't have *that* excitement. He was out of town, and was not to come home till six o'clock.

It was an awfully hot day. The sun just beat down, and there was n't a breath of air. By noon I was simply crazy with my stuffy, long-sleeved, high-necked blue gingham dress and my great clumpy shoes. It seemed all of a sudden as if I could n't stand it — not another minute — not

a single minute more — to be Mary, I mean.
And suddenly I determined that for a while, just
a little while, I'd be Marie again. Why could n't
I? There was n't anybody going to be there but
just myself, *all day long.*

I ran then upstairs to the guest-room closet
where Aunt Jane had made me put all my Marie dresses and things when the Mary ones came.
Well, I got out the very fluffiest, softest white
dress there was there, and the little white slippers and the silk stockings that I loved, and the
blue silk sash, and the little gold locket and chain
that Mother gave me that Aunt Jane would n't
let me wear. And I dressed up. My, did n't I
dress up? And I just *threw* those old heavy shoes
and black cotton stockings into the corner, and
the blue gingham dress after them (though Mary
went right away and picked the dress up, and
hung it in the closet, of course); but I had the fun
of throwing it, anyway.

Oh, how good those Marie things did feel to
Mary's hot, tired flesh and bones, and how I did
dance and sing around the room in those light
little slippers! Then Susie rang the dinner-bell
and I went down to the dining-room feeling like
a really truly young lady, I can tell you.

Susie stared, of course, and said, "My, how
fine we are to-day!" But I did n't mind Susie.

After dinner I went out into the hall and I

sang; I sang all over the house. And I ran upstairs and I ran down; and I jumped all the last
three steps, even if it was so warm. Then I went
into the parlor and played every lively thing
that I could think of on the piano. And I sang
there, too — silly little songs that Marie used to
sing to Lester. And I tried to think I was really
down there to Boston, singing to Lester; and that
Mother was right in the next room waiting for
me.

Then I stopped and turned around on the
piano-stool. And there was the coffin plate, and
the wax cross, and the hair wreath; and the
room was just as still as death. And I knew I
was n't in Boston. I was there in Andersonville.
And there was n't any Baby Lester there, nor any
mother waiting for me in the next room. And all
the fluffy white dresses and silk stockings in the
world would n't make me Marie. I was really
just Mary, and I had got to have three whole
months more of it.

And then is when I began to cry. And I cried
just as hard as I 'd been singing a minute before.
I was on the floor with my head in my arms on
the piano-stool when Father's voice came to me
from the doorway.

"Mary, Mary, what in the world does this
mean?"

I jumped up and stood "at attention," the way

you have to, of course, when fathers speak to you. I could n't help showing I had been crying — he had seen it. But I tried very hard to stop now. My first thought, after my startled realization that he was there, was to wonder how long he had been there — how much of all that awful singing and banging he had heard.

"Yes, sir." I tried not to have my voice shake as I said it; but I could n't quite help that.

"What is the meaning of this, Mary? Why are you crying?"

I shook my head. I did n't want to tell him, of course; so I just stammered out something about being sorry I had disturbed him. Then I edged toward the door to show him that if he would step one side I would go away at once and not bother him any longer.

But he did n't step one side. He asked more questions, one right after another.

"Are you sick, Mary?"

I shook my head.

"Did you hurt yourself?"

I shook my head again.

"It is n't — your mother — you have n't had bad news from her?"

And then I blurted it out without thinking — without thinking at all what I was saying: "No, no — but I wish I had, I wish I had; 'cause then

I could go to her, and go away from here!"
The minute I'd said it I *knew* what I'd said,
and how awful it sounded; and I clapped my fingers to my lips. But 't was too late. It's always
too late, when you've once said it. So I just
waited for him to thunder out his anger; for, of
course, I thought he *would* thunder in rage and
righteous indignation.

But he did n't. Instead, very quietly and gently
he said:

"Are you so unhappy, then, Mary — here?"

And I looked at him, and his eyes and his
mouth and his whole face were n't angry at all.
They were just sorry, actually sorry. And somehow, before I knew it, I was crying again, and
Father, with his arm around me — *with his arm
around me!* think of that! — was leading me to
the sofa.

And I cried and cried there, with my head on
the arm of the sofa, till I'd made a big tear spot
on the linen cover; and I wondered if it would
dry up before Aunt Jane saw it, or if it would
change color or leak through to the red plush
underneath, or some other dreadful thing. And
then, some way, I found myself telling it all over
to Father — about Mary and Marie, I mean,
just as if he was Mother, or some one I loved —
I mean, some one I loved and *was n't afraid of;*
for of course I love Father. Of course I do!

Well, I told him everything (when I got started there was no stopping) — all about how hard it was to be Mary, and how to-day I had tried to be Marie for just a little while, to rest me. He interrupted here, and wanted to know if that was why I looked so different to-day — more as I had when I first came; and I said yes, that these were Marie things that Mary could n't wear. And when he asked, "Why, pray?" in a voice almost cross, I told him, of course, that Aunt Jane would n't let me; that Mary had to wear brown serge and calfskin boots that were durable, and that would wear well.

And when I told him how sorry I was about the music and such a noise as I'd been making, he asked if *that* was Marie's fault, too; and I said yes, of course — that Aunt Jane did n't like to have Mary play at all, except hymns and funeral marches, and Mary did n't know any. And he grunted a queer little grunt, and said, "Well, well, upon my soul, upon my soul!" Then he said, "Go on." And I did go on.

I told him how I was afraid it *was* going to be just like Dr. Jekyll and Mr. Hyde. (I forgot to say I've read it now. I found it in Father's library.) Of course not *just* like it, only one of me was going to be bad, and one good, I was afraid, if I did n't look out. I told him how Marie always wanted to kick up rugs, and move the chairs out of their sockets in the carpet, and leave books around handy, and such things. And so to-day it seemed as if I'd just got to have a vacation from Mary's hot gingham dresses and clumpy shoes. And I told him how lonesome I was without anybody, not *anybody*; and I told about Charlie Smith and Paul Mayhew and Mr. Claude Livingstone, and how Aunt Jane would n't let me have them, either, even if I was standing where the brook and river meet.

Father gave another funny little grunt here, and got up suddenly and walked over to the window. I thought at first he was angry; but he was n't. He was even more gentle when he came back and sat down again, and he seemed interested, very much interested in everything I told him. But I stopped just in time from saying again how I wished I could go back to Boston; but I'm not sure but he knew I was going to say it.

But he was very nice and kind and told me not to worry about the music — that he did n't mind it at all. He'd been in several times and heard it. And I thought almost, by the way he spoke, that he'd come in on purpose to hear it; but I guess that was a mistake. He just put it that way so I would n't worry over it — about its bothering him, I mean.

He was going to say more, maybe; but I don't know. I had to run. I heard Aunt Jane's voice on the piazza saying good-bye to the lady that had brought her home; so, of course, I had to run and hang Marie in the closet and get out Mary from the corner before she saw me. And I did.

By dinner-time I had on the gingham dress and the hot clumpy shoes again; and I had washed my face in cold water so I had got most of the tear spots off. I did n't want Aunt Jane to see them and ask questions, of course. And I guess she did n't. Anyway, she did n't say anything.

Father did n't say anything either, but he acted queer. Aunt Jane tried to tell him something about the missionary meeting and the heathen, and a great famine that was raging. At first he did n't say anything; then he said, oh, yes, to be sure, how very interesting, and he was glad, very glad. And Aunt Jane was so disgusted, and accused him of being even more absent-minded than usual, which was entirely unnecessary, she said.

But even that did n't move Father a mite. He just said, yes, yes, very likely; and went on scowling to himself and stirring his coffee after he'd drank it all up — I mean, stirring where it had been in the cup.

I did n't know but after supper he'd speak to me and ask me to come to the library. I *hoped* he would. There were lots more things I'd like to have said to him. But he did n't. He never said a

word. He just kept scowling, and got up from the
table and went off by himself. But he did n't
go out to the observatory, as he most generally
does. He went into the library and shut the
door.

He was there when the telephone message came
at eight o'clock. And what do you think? He'd
forgotten he was going to speak before the College
Astronomy Club that evening! Forgotten his old
stars for once. I don't know why. I did think, for
a minute, 't was 'cause of me — what I'd told
him. But I knew, of course, right away that it
could n't be that. He'd never forget his stars for
me! Probably he was just reading up about some
other stars, or had forgotten how late it was, or
something. (Father's always forgetting things.)
But, anyway, when Aunt Jane called him he got
his hat and hurried off without so much as one
word to me, who was standing near, or to Aunt
Jane, who was following him all through the hall,
and telling him in her most I'm-amazed-at-you
voice how shockingly absent-minded he was getting to be.

One week later.

Father's been awfully queer this whole week
through. I can't make him out at all. Sometimes
I think he's glad I told him all those things in the
parlor that day I dressed up in Marie's things,

and sometimes I think he's sorry and wished I had n't.

The very next morning he came down to breakfast with such a funny look on his face. He said good-morning to me three times, and all through breakfast he kept looking over at me with a kind of scowl that was not cross at all — just puzzled.

After breakfast he did n't go out to the observatory, not even into the library. He fidgeted around the dining-room till Aunt Jane went out into the kitchen to give her orders to Susie; then he burst out, all of a sudden:

"Well, Mary, what shall we do to-day?" Just like that he said it, as if we'd been doing things together every day of our lives.

"D-do?" I asked; and I know I showed how surprised I was by the way I stammered and flushed up.

"Certainly, do," he answered, impatient and scowling. "What shall we do?"

"Why, Father, I — I don't know," I stammered again.

"Come, come, of course you know!" he cried. "You know what you want to do, don't you?"

I shook my head. I was so astonished I could n't even think. And when you can't think you certainly can't talk.

"Nonsense, Mary," scowled Father again. "Of course you know what you want to do! What are

you in the habit of doing with your young friends
— your Carries and Charlies, and all the rest?"

I guess I just stood and stared and did n't say
anything; for after a minute he cried: "Well —
well — well? I'm waiting."

"Why, we — we walk — and talk — and play
games," I began; but right away he interrupted.

"Good! Very well, then, we'll walk. I'm not
Carrie or Charlie, but I believe I can walk and
talk — perhaps even play games. Who knows?
Come, get your hat."

And I got my hat, and we went.

But what a funny, funny walk that was! He
meant to make it a good one; I know he did.
And he tried. He tried real hard. But he walked
so fast I could n't half keep up with him; then,
when he saw how I was hurrying, he'd slow
down, 'way down, and look so worried — till he'd
forget and go striding off again, 'way ahead of me.

We went up on the hill through the Benton
woods, and it was perfectly lovely up there. He
did n't say much at first. Then, all of a sudden,
he began to talk, about anything and everything.
And I knew, by the way he did it, that he'd just
happened to think he'd got to talk.

And how he talked! He asked me was I warmly
clad (and here it is August!), and did I have a
good breakfast, and how old was I, and did I
enjoy my studies — which shows how little he

was really thinking what he was saying. He
knows school closed ages ago. Was n't he teaching me himself the last of it, too? All around us
were flowers and birds, and oh, so many, many
lovely things. But he never said a word about
them. He just talked — because he 'd got to talk.
I knew it, and it made me laugh inside, though
all the while it made me sort of want to cry, too.
Funny, was n't it?

After a time he did n't talk any more, but just
walked on and on; and by and by we came home.

Of course, it was n't awfully jolly — that walk
was n't; and I guess Father did n't think it was
either. Anyhow, he has n't asked me to go again
this week, and he looked tired and worried and
sort of discouraged when he got back from that
one.

But he 's asked me to do other things. The
next day after the walk he asked me to play to
him. Yes, he *asked* me to; and he went into the
parlor and sat down on one of the chairs and
listened while I played three pieces. Of course,
I did n't play loud ones, nor very fast ones, and
I was so scared I 'm afraid I did n't play them
very well. But he was very polite and said,
"Thank you, Mary," and, "That that was very
nice"; then he stood up and said, "Thank you"
again and went away into the library, very
polite, but stiff, like company.

The next evening he took me out to the observatory to see the stars. That was lovely. Honestly I had a perfectly beautiful time, and I think Father did, too. He was n't stiff and polite one bit. Oh, I don't mean that he was *im*-polite or rude. It's just that he was n't stiff as if I was company. And he was so happy with his stars and his telescope, and so glad to show them to me — oh, I had a beautiful time, and I told him so; and he looked real pleased. But Aunt Jane came for me before I'd had half enough, and I had to go to bed.

The next morning I thought he'd be different, somehow, because we'd had such a lovely time together the night before. But he was n't. He just said, "Good-morning, Mary," and began to read his paper. And he read his paper all through breakfast without saying another word to me. Then he got up and went into the library, and I never saw him again all day except at dinner-time and supper-time, and *then* he did n't talk to me.

But after supper he took me out again to see the stars, and he was just as nice and friendly as could be. Not a bit like a man that's only a father by order of the court. But the next day —!

Well — and that's the way it's been all the week. And that's why I say he's been so queer. One minute he'll be just as nice and folksy as you could ask anybody to be, and the very next he's looking right through you as if he did n't see you at all, and you wonder and wonder what's the matter, and if you've done anything to displease him.

Sometimes he seems almost glad and happy, and then he'll look so sorry and sad!

I just can't understand my father at all.

Another week later.

I'm so excited I don't know what to do. The most wonderful thing has happened. I can't hardly believe it yet myself. Yet it's so. My trunk is all packed, and I'm to go home to-morrow. *To-morrow!*

This is the way it happened.

Mother wrote Aunt Jane and asked if I might not be allowed to come home for the opening of school in September. She said she understood quite well that she had no *right* to ask this, and, of course, if they saw fit, they were entirely within their rights to refuse to allow me to go until the allotted time. But that she could not help asking it for my sake, on account of the benefit to be derived from being there at the opening of the school year.

Of course, I did n't know Mother was going to write this. But she knew all about the school here, and how I came out, and everything. I've always told Mother everything that has happened. Oh, of course, I have n't written "every few minutes," as she asked me to. (That was a joke, anyway, of course.) But I have written every few days, and, as I said before, I told her everything.

Well, when the letter came I took it to Aunt Jane myself; and I was *crazy* to know what was in it, for I recognized the writing, of course. But Aunt Jane did n't tell me. She opened it, read it, kind of flushed up, and said, "Humph! The idea!" under her breath, and put the letter in her pocket.

Marie wanted to make a scene and insist on knowing what was in her own mother's letter; but Mary contented herself with looking superb and haughty and disdainful, and marching out of the room without giving Aunt Jane the satisfaction of even being asked what was in that letter.

But at the table that noon Aunt Jane read it to Father out loud. So that's how I came to know just what was in it. She started first to hand it over to him to read; but as he put out his hand to take it I guess he saw the handwriting, for he drew back quickly, looking red and queer.

"From Mrs. Anderson to you?" he asked. And when Aunt Jane nodded her head he sat still farther back in his chair and said, with a little wave of his hand, "I never care to read — other people's letters."

Aunt Jane said, "Stuff and nonsense, Charles, don't be silly!" But she pulled back the letter and read it — after giving a kind of an uneasy glance in my direction.

Father never looked up once while she was reading it. He kept his eyes on his plate and the baked beans he was eating. I watched him. You see, I knew, by Aunt Jane's reading the letter to him, that it was something he had got to decide; and when I found out what it was, of course, I was just crazy. I wanted to go so. So I watched Father's face to see if he was going to let me go. But I could n't make out. I could n't make out at all. It changed — oh, yes, it changed a great deal as she read; but I could n't make out what kind of a change it was at all.

Aunt Jane finished the letter and began to fold it up. I could see she was waiting for Father to speak; but he never said a word. He kept right on — eating beans.

Then Aunt Jane cleared her throat and spoke.

"You will not let her go, of course, Charles; but naturally I had to read the letter to you. I will write to Mrs. Anderson to-night."

Father looked up then.

"Yes," he said quietly; "and you may tell her, please, that Mary *will* go."

"Charles!"

Aunt Jane said that. But I — I almost ran

around the table and hugged him. (Oh, how I wish he was the kind of a father you could do that to!)

"Charles!" said Aunt Jane again. "Surely you are n't going to give in so tamely as this to that child and her mother!"

"I'm not giving in at all, Jane," said Father, very quietly again. "I am consulting my own wishes in the matter. I prefer to have her go."

I 'most cried out then. Some way, it *hurt* to have him say it like that, right out — that he *wanted* me to go. You see, I'd begun to think he was getting so he did n't mind so very much having me here. All the last two weeks he'd been different, really different. But more of that anon. I'll go on with what happened at the table. And, as I said, I did feel bad to have him speak like that. And I can remember now just how the lump came right up in my throat.

Then Aunt Jane spoke, stiff and dignified.

"Oh, very well, of course, if you put it that way. I can quite well understand that you would want her to go — for *your* sake. But I thought that, under the circumstances, you would manage somehow to put up with the noise and — "

"Jane!" Just like that he interrupted, and he thundered, too, so that Aunt Jane actually jumped. And I guess I did, too. He had sprung to his feet. "Jane, let us close this matter once for all. I am not letting the child go for *my* sake. I am letting her go for her own. So far as I am concerned, if I consulted no one's wishes but my own, I should — keep her here always."

With that he turned and strode from the room, leaving Aunt Jane and me just staring after him.

But only for a minute did *I* stare. It came to me then what he had said — that he would like to keep me here *always*. For I had heard it, even if he had said the last word very low, and in a queer, indistinct voice. I was sure I had heard it, and I suddenly realized what it meant. So I ran after him; and that time, if I had found him, I think I *would* have hugged him. But I did n't find him. He must have gone quite away from the house. He was n't even out to the observatory. I went out to see.

He did n't come in all the afternoon. I watched for that, too. And when he did come — well, I would n't have dared to hug him then. He had his very sternest I-am-not-thinking-of-you-at-all air, and he just came in to supper and then went into the library without saying hardly anything. Yet, some way, the look on his face made me cry. I don't know why.

The next day he was more as he has been since we had that talk in the parlor. And he *has* been different since then, you know. He really has. He has talked quite a lot with me, as I have said, and

I think he's been trying, part of the time, to find something I'll be interested in. Honestly, I think he's been trying to make up for Carrie Heywood and Stella Mayhew and Charlie Smith and Mr. Livingstone. I think that's why he took me to walk that day in the woods, and why he took me out to the observatory to see the stars quite a number of times. Twice he's asked me to play to him, and once he asked me if Mary wasn't about ready to dress up in Marie's clothes again. But he was joking then, I knew, for Aunt Jane was right there in the house. Besides, I saw the twinkle in his eyes that I've seen there once or twice before. I just love that twinkle in Father's eyes!

But that hasn't come any since Mother's letter to Aunt Jane arrived. He's been the same in one way, yet different in another. Honestly, if it didn't seem too wildly absurd for anything, I should say he was actually sorry to have me go. But, of course, that isn't possible. Oh, yes, I know he said that day at the dinner-table that he should like to keep me always. But I don't think he really meant it. He hasn't acted a mite like that since, and I guess he said it just to hush up Aunt Jane, and make her stop arguing the matter.

Anyway, I'm *going* to-morrow. And I'm so excited I can hardly breathe.

CHAPTER VI

WHEN I AM BOTH TOGETHER

BOSTON AGAIN.

Well, I came last night. Mother and Grandfather and Aunt Hattie and Baby Lester all met me at the station. And, my! was n't I glad to see them? Well, I just guess I was!

I was specially glad on account of having such a dreadful time with Father that morning. I mean, I was feeling specially lonesome and homesick, and not-belonging-anywhere like.

You see, it was this way: I'd been sort of hoping, I know, that at the last, when I came to really go, Father would get back the understanding smile and the twinkle, and show that he really *did* care for me, and was sorry to have me go. But, dear me! Why, he never was so stern and solemn, and you 're-my-daughter-only-by-the-order-of-the-court sort of way as he was that morning.

He never even spoke at the breakfast-table. (He was n't there hardly long enough to speak, anyway, and he never ate a thing, only his coffee — I mean he drank it.) Then he pushed his chair back from the table and stalked out of the room.

He went to the station with me; but he did n't

talk there much, only to ask if I was sure I had n't forgotten anything, and was I warmly clad. Warmly clad, indeed! And there it was still August, and hot as it could be! But that only goes to show how absent-minded he was, and how little he was really thinking of *me!*

Well, of course, he got my ticket and checked my trunk, and did all those proper, necessary things; then we sat down to wait for the train. But did he stay with me and talk to me and tell me how glad he had been to have me with him, and how sorry he was to have me go, and all the other nice, polite things 'most everybody thinks they've got to say when a visitor goes away? He did not. He asked me again if I was sure I had not left anything, and was I warmly clad; then he took out his newspaper and began to read. That is, he pretended to read; but I don't believe he read much, for he never turned the sheet once; and twice, when I looked at him, he was looking fixedly at me, as if he was thinking of something. So I guess he was just pretending to read, so he would n't have to talk to me.

But he did n't even do that long, for he got up and went over and looked at a map hanging on the wall opposite, and at a big time-table near the other corner. Then he looked at his watch again with a won't-that-train-ever-come? air, and walked back to me and sat down.

And how do you suppose *I* felt, to have him act like that before all those people — to show so plainly that he was just longing to have me go? I guess he was n't any more anxious for that train to come than *I* was. And it did seem as if it never would come, too. And it did n't come for ages. It was ten minutes late.

Oh, I did so hope he would n't go down to the junction. It's so hard to be taken care of "because it's my duty, you know"! But he went. I told him he need n't, when he was getting on the train with me. I told him I just knew I could do it beautifully all by myself, almost-a-young lady like me. But he only put his lips together hard, and said, cold, like ice: "Are you then so eager to be rid of me?" Just as if *I* was the one that was eager to get rid of somebody!

Well, as I said, he went. But he was n't much better on the train than he had been in the station. He was as nervous and fidgety as a witch, and he acted as if he did so wish it would be over, and over quick. But at the junction — at the junction a funny thing happened. He put me on the train, just as Mother had done, and spoke to the conductor. (How I hated to have him do that! Why, I 'm six whole months older, 'most, than I was when I went up there!) And then, when he 'd put me in my seat (Father, I mean; not the conductor), all of a sudden he leaned over and kissed me; *kissed me — Father!* Then, before I could speak, or even look at him, he was gone; and I did n't see him again, though it must have been five whole minutes before that train went.

I had a nice trip down to Boston, though nothing much happened. This conductor was not near so nice and polite as the one I had coming up; and there was n't any lady with a baby to play with, nor any nice young gentleman to loan me magazines or buy candy for me. But it was n't a very long ride from the junction to Boston, anyway. So I did n't mind. Besides, I knew I had Mother waiting for me.

And was n't I glad to get there? Well, I just guess I was! And *they* acted as if they were glad to see me — Mother, Grandfather, Aunt Hattie, and even Baby Lester. He knew me, and remembered me. He'd grown a lot, too. And they said I had, and that I looked very nice. (I forgot to say that, of course, I had put on the Marie clothes to come home in — though I honestly think Aunt Jane wanted to send me home in Mary's blue gingham and calfskin shoes. As if I'd have appeared in Boston in *that* rig!)

My, but it was good to get into an automobile again and just *go!* And it was so good to have folks around you dressed in something

besides don't-care black alpaca and stiff collars.
And I said so. And Mother seemed so pleased.

"You did want to come back to me, darling,
did n't you?" she cried, giving me a little hug.
And she looked so happy when I told her all
over again how good it seemed to be Marie again,
and have her and Boston, and automobiles, and
pretty dresses and folks and noise again.

She did n't say anything about Father then;
but later, when we were up in my pretty room
alone, and I was taking off my things, she made
me tell her that Father *had n't* won my love
away from her, and that I *did n't* love him better
than I did her; and that I *would n't* rather stay
with him than with her.

Then she asked me a lot of questions about
what I did there, and Aunt Jane, and how she
looked, and Father, and was he as fond of stars
as ever (though she must have known 'most
everything, 'cause I'd already written it, but she
asked me just the same). And she seemed real
interested in everything I told her.

And she asked was he lonesome; and I told her
no, I did n't think so; and that, anyway, he could
have all the ladies' company he wanted by just
being around when they called. And when she
asked what I meant, I told her about Mrs. Darling, and the rest, and how they came evenings
and Sundays, and how Father did n't like them,

but would flee to the observatory. And she laughed and looked funny, for a minute. But right away she changed and looked very sober, with the kind of expression she has when she stands up in church and says the Apostles' Creed on Sunday; only this time she said she was very sorry, she was sure; that she hoped my father would find some estimable woman who would make a good home for him.

Then the dinner-gong sounded, and she did n't say any more.

There was company that evening. The violinist. He brought his violin, and he and Mother played a whole hour together. He 's awfully handsome. I think he 's lovely. Oh, I do so hope he 's *the* one! Anyhow, I hope there 's *some* one. I don't want this novel to all fizzle out without there being *any* one to make it a love story! Besides, as I said before, I 'm particularly anxious that Mother shall find somebody to marry her, so she 'll stop being divorced, anyway.

A month later.

Yes, I know it 's been *ages* since I 've written here in this book; but there just has n't been a minute's time.

First, of course, school began, and I had to attend to that. And, of course, I had to tell the girls all about Andersonville — except the parts

I did n't want to tell, about Stella Mayhew, and
my coming out of school. I did n't tell *that*. And
right here let me say how glad I was to get back
to this school — a real school — so different from
that one up in Andersonville! For that matter,
everything's different here from what it is in
Andersonville. I'd so much rather be Marie than
Mary. I know I won't ever be Dr. Jekyll and
Mr. Hyde here. I'll be the good one all the
time.

It's funny how much easier it is to be good in
silk stockings and a fluffy white dress than it is in
blue gingham and calfskin. Oh, I'll own up that
Marie forgets sometimes and says things Mary
used to say; like calling Olga a hired girl instead
of a maid, as Aunt Hattie wants, and saying dinner instead of luncheon at noon, and some other
things.

I heard Aunt Hattie tell Mother one day that
it was going to take about the whole six months
to break Mary Marie of those outlandish country ways of hers. (So, you see, it is n't all honey
and pie even for Marie. This trying to be Mary
and Marie, even six months apart, is n't the easiest thing ever was!) I don't think Mother liked
it very well — what Aunt Hattie said about my
outlandish ways. I did n't hear all Mother said,
but I knew by the way she looked and acted, and
the little I did hear, that she did n't care for that

word "outlandish" applied to her little girl — not at all.

Mother's a dear. And she's so happy! And, by the way, I think it *is* the violinist. He's here a lot, and she's out with him to concerts and plays, and riding in his automobile. And she always puts on her prettiest dresses, and she's very particular about her shoes, and her hats, that they're becoming, and all that. Oh, I'm so excited! And I'm having such a good time watching them! Oh, I don't mean watching them in a disagreeable way, so that they *see* it; and, of course, I don't listen — not the sneak kind of listening. But, of course, I have to get all I can — for the book, you know; and, of course, if I just happen to be in the window-seat corner in the library and hear things accidentally, why, that's all right.

And I have heard things.

He says her eyes are lovely. He likes her best in blue. He's very lonely, and he never found a woman before who really understood him. He thinks her soul and his are tuned to the same string. (Oh, dear! That sounds funny and horrid, and not at all the way it did when *he* said it. It was beautiful then. But — well, that is what it meant, anyway.)

She told him she was lonely, too, and that she was very glad to have him for a friend; and he said he prized her friendship above everything else in the world. And he looks at her, and follows her around the room with his eyes; and she blushes up real pink and pretty lots of times when he comes into the room.

Now, if that is n't making love to each other, I don't know what *is*. I'm sure he's going to propose. Oh, I'm so excited!

Oh, yes, I know if he does propose and she says yes, he'll be my new father. I understand that. And, of course, I can't help wondering how I'll like it. Sometimes I think I won't like it at all. Sometimes I almost catch myself wishing that I did n't have to have any new father or mother. I'd *never* need a new mother, anyway, and I would n't need a new father if my father-by-order-of-the-court would be as nice as he was there two or three times in the observatory.

But, there! After all, I must remember that I'm not the one that's doing the choosing. It's Mother. And if she wants the violinist I must n't have anything to say. Besides, I really like him very much, anyway. He's the best of the lot, I'm sure of that. And that's something. And then, of course, I'm glad to have something to make this a love story, and best of all I would be glad to have Mother stop being divorced, anyway.

Mr. Harlow does n't come here any more, I guess. Anyway, I have n't seen him here once since I came back; and I have n't heard anybody mention his name.

Quite a lot of the others are here, and there are some new ones. But the violinist is here most, and Mother seems to go out with him most to places. That's why I say I think it's the violinist.

I have n't heard from Father.

Now just my writing that down that way shows that I *expected* to hear from him, though I don't really see why I should, either. Of course, he never *has* written to me; and, of course, I understand that I'm nothing but his daughter by order of the court. But, some way, I did think maybe he'd write me just a little bit of a note in answer to mine — my bread-and-butter letter, I mean; for of course, Mother had me write that to him as soon as I got here.

But he has n't.

I wonder how he's getting along, and if he misses me any. But of course, he does n't do *that*. If I was a star, now —!

Two days after Thanksgiving.

The violinist has got a rival. I'm sure he has. It's Mr. Easterbrook. He's old — much as forty — and bald-headed and fat, and has got lots of money. And he's a very estimable man. (I heard Aunt Hattie say that.) He's awfully jolly, and I like him. He brings me the loveliest boxes of

candy, and calls me Puss. (I don't like *that*, particularly. I'd prefer him to call me Miss Anderson.) He's not nearly so good-looking as the violinist. The violinist is lots more thrilling, but I
should n't wonder if Mr. Easterbrook was more
comfortable to live with.

The violinist is the kind of a man that makes
you want to sit up and take notice, and have your
hair and finger nails and shoes just right; but
with Mr. Easterbrook you would n't mind a bit
sitting in a big chair before the fire with a pair
of old slippers on, if your feet were tired.

Mr. Easterbrook does n't care for music. He's
a broker. He looks awfully bored when the violinist is playing, and he fidgets with his watch-
chain, and clears his throat very loudly just before he speaks every time. His automobile is
bigger and handsomer than the violinist's. (Aunt
Hattie says the violinist's automobile is a hired
one.) And Mr. Easterbrook's flowers that he sends
to Mother are handsomer, too, and lots more of
them, than the violinist's. Aunt Hattie has noticed that, too. In fact, I guess there is n't anything about Mr. Easterbrook that she does n't
notice.

Aunt Hattie likes Mr. Easterbrook lots better
than she does the violinist. I heard her talking
to Mother one day. She said that any one that
would look twice at a lazy, shiftless fiddler with

probably not a dollar laid by for a rainy day, when all the while there was just waiting to be picked an estimable gentleman of independent fortune and stable position like Mr. Easterbrook — well, she had her opinion of her; that's all. She meant Mother, of course. *I* knew that. I'm no child.

Mother knew it, too; and she did n't like it. She flushed up and bit her lip, and answered back, cold, like ice.

"I understand, of course, what you mean, Hattie; but even if I acknowledged that this very estimable, unimpeachable gentleman was waiting to be picked (which I do not), I should have to remind you that I've already had one experience with an estimable, unimpeachable gentleman of independent fortune and stable position, and I do not care for another."

"But, my dear Madge," began Aunt Hattie again, "to marry a man without *any* money —"

"I have n't married him yet," cut in Mother, cold again, like ice. "But let me tell you this, Hattie. I'd rather live on bread and water in a log cabin with the man I loved than in a palace with an estimable, unimpeachable gentleman who gave me the shivers every time he came into the room."

And it was just after she said this that I interrupted. I was right in plain sight in the window-

seat reading; but I guess they'd forgotten I was
there, for they both jumped a lot when I spoke.
And yet I'll leave it to you if what I said was n't
perfectly natural.

"Of course, you would, Mother!" I cried.
"And, anyhow, if you did marry the violinist,
and you found out afterward you did n't like
him, that would n't matter a mite, for you could
*un*marry him at any time, just as you did Father,
and —"

But they would n't let me finish. They would
n't let me say anything more. Mother cried, "*Marie!*" in her most I'm-shocked-at-you voice; and
Aunt Hattie cried, "Child — child!" And she
seemed shocked, too. And both of them threw
up their hands and looked at each other in the
did-you-ever-hear such a dreadful-thing? way
that old folks do when young folks have displeased them. And then they both went right out
of the room, talking about the unfortunate effect
on a child's mind, and perverted morals, and
Mother reproaching Aunt Hattie for talking
about those things before that child (meaning
me, of course). Then they got too far down the
hall for me to hear any more. But I don't see why
they needed to have made such a fuss. It was n't
any secret that Mother got a divorce; and if she
got one once, of course she could again. (That's
what I'm going to do when I'm married, if I

grow tired of him — my husband, I mean.) Oh, yes, I know Mrs. Mayhew and her crowd don't seem to think divorces are very nice; but there need n't anybody try to make me think that anything my mother does is n't perfectly nice and all right. And *she* got a divorce. So, there!

One week later.

There has n't much happened — only one or two things. But maybe I'd better tell them before I forget it, especially as they have a good deal to do with the love part of the story. And I'm always so glad to get anything of that kind. I've been so afraid this would n't be much of a love story, after all. But I guess it will be, all right. Anyhow, I *know* Mother's part will be, for it's getting more and more exciting — about Mr. Easterbrook and the violinist, I mean.

They both want Mother. Anybody can see that now, and, of course, Mother sees it. But which she 'll take I don't know. Nobody knows. It's perfectly plain to be seen, though, which one Grandfather and Aunt Hattie want her to take! It 's Mr. Easterbrook.

And he is awfully nice. He brought me a perfectly beautiful bracelet the other day — but Mother would n't let me keep it. So he had to take it back. I don't think he liked it very well, and I did n't like it, either. I *wanted* that bracelet.

But Mother says I'm much too young to wear much jewelry. Oh, will the time ever come when I'll be old enough to take my proper place in the world? Sometimes it seems as if it never would!

Well, as I said, it's plain to be seen who it is that Grandfather and Aunt Hattie favor; but I'm not so sure about Mother. Mother acts funny. Sometimes she won't go with either of them anywhere; then she seems to want to go all the time. And she acts as if she didn't care which she went with, so long as she was just going — somewhere. I think, though, she really likes the violinist the best; and I guess Grandfather and Aunt Hattie think so, too.

Something happened last night. Grandfather began to talk at the dinner-table. He'd heard something he didn't like about the violinist, I guess, and he started in to tell Mother. But they stopped him. Mother and Aunt Hattie looked at him and then at me, and then back to him, in their most see-who's-here! — you-mustn't-talk-before-her way. So he shrugged his shoulders and stopped.

But I guess he told them in the library afterwards, for I heard them all talking very excitedly, and some loud; and I guess Mother didn't like what they said, and got quite angry, for I heard her say, when she came out through the door, that she didn't believe a word of it, and she thought it was a wicked, cruel shame to tell stories like that just because they did n't like a man.

This morning she broke an engagement with Mr. Easterbrook to go auto-riding and went with the violinist to a morning musicale instead; and after she'd gone Aunt Hattie sighed and looked at Grandfather and shrugged her shoulders, and said she was afraid they'd driven her straight into the arms of the one they wanted to avoid, and that Madge always *would* take the part of the under dog.

I suppose they thought I would n't understand. But I did, perfectly. They meant that by telling stories about the violinist they'd been hoping to get her to give him up, but instead of that, they'd made her turn to him all the more, just because she was so sorry for him.

Funny, is n't it?

One week later.

Well, I guess now something has happened all right! And let me say right away that *I* don't like that violinist now, either, any better than Grandfather and Aunt Hattie. And it's not entirely because of what happened last night, either. It's been coming on for quite a while — ever since I first saw him talking to Theresa in the hall when she let him in one night a week ago.

Theresa is awfully pretty, and I guess he thinks so. Anyhow, I heard him telling her so in the hall, and she laughed and blushed and looked sideways at him. Then they saw me, and he stiffened up and said, very proper and dignified, "Kindly hand my card to Mrs. Anderson." And Theresa said, "Yes, sir." And she was very proper and dignified, too.

Well, that was the beginning. I can see now that it was, though I never thought of its meaning anything then, only that he thought Theresa was a pretty girl, just as we all do.

But four days ago I saw them again. He tried to put his arm around her that time, and the very next day he tried to kiss her, and after a minute she let him. More than once, too. And last night I heard him tell her she was the dearest girl in all the world, and he'd be perfectly happy if he could only marry her.

Well, you can imagine how I felt, when I thought all the time it was Mother he was coming to see! And now to find out that it was Theresa he wanted all the time, and he was only coming to see Mother so he could see Theresa!

At first I was angry, — just plain angry; and I was frightened, too, for I couldn't help worrying about Mother — for fear she would mind, you know, when she found out that it was Theresa that he cared for, after all. I remembered what a lot Mother had been with him, and the pretty dresses and hats she'd put on for him, and all that. And I thought how she'd broken engagements with Mr. Easterbrook to go with him, and it made me angry all over again. And I thought how *mean* it was of him to use poor Mother as a kind of shield to hide his courting of Theresa! I was angry, too, to have my love story all spoiled, when I was getting along so beautifully with Mother and the violinist.

But I'm feeling better now. I've been thinking it over. I don't believe Mother's going to care so very much. I don't believe she'd *want* a man that would pretend to come courting her, when all the while he was really courting the hired girl — I mean maid. Besides, there's Mr. Easterbrook left (and one or two others that I have n't said much about, as I did n't think they had much chance). And so far as the love story for the book is concerned, *that* is n't spoiled, after all, for it will be ever so much more exciting to have the violinist fall in love with Theresa than with Mother, for, of course, Theresa is n't in the same station of life at all, and that makes it a — a mess-alliance. (I don't remember exactly what that word is; but I know it means an alliance that makes a mess of things because the lovers are not equal to each other.) Of course, for the folks who have to live it, it may not be so nice;

but for my story here this makes it all the more romantic and thrilling. So *that's* all right.

Of course, so far, I'm the only one that knows, for I have n't told it, and I'm the only one that's seen anything. Of course, I shall warn Mother, if I think it's necessary, so she'll understand it is n't her, but Theresa, that the violinist is really in love with and courting. *She* won't mind, I'm sure, after she thinks of it a minute. And won't it be a good joke on Aunt Hattie and Grandfather when they find out they've been fooled all the time, supposing it's Mother, and worrying about it?

Oh, I don't know! This is some love story, after all!

Two days later.

Well, I should say it was! What do you suppose has happened now? Why, that wretched violinist is nothing but a deep-dyed villain! Listen what he did. He proposed to Mother — actually proposed to her — and after all he'd said to that Theresa girl, about his being perfectly happy if he could marry *her*. And Mother — Mother all the time not knowing! Oh, I'm so glad I was there to rescue her! I don't mean at the proposal — I did n't hear that. But afterward.

It was like this.

They had been out automobiling — Mother and the violinist. He came for her at three o'clock. He said it was a beautiful warm day, and maybe the last one they'd have this year; and she must go. And she went.

I was in my favorite window-seat, reading, when they came home and walked into the library. They never looked my way at all, but just walked toward the fireplace. And there he took hold of both her hands and said:

"Why must you wait, darling? Why can't you give me my answer now, and make me the happiest man in all the world?"

"Yes, yes, I know," answered Mother; and I knew by her voice that she was all shaky and trembly. "But if I could only be sure — sure of myself."

"But, dearest, you're sure of me!" cried the violinist. "You *know* how I love you. You know you're the only woman I have ever loved, or ever could love!"

Yes, just like that he said it — that awful lie — and to my mother. My stars! Do you suppose I waited to hear any more? I guess not!

I fairly tumbled off my seat, and my book dropped with a bang, as I ran forward. Dear, dear, but how they did jump — both of them! And I guess they *were* surprised. I never thought how 't was going to affect them — my breaking

"WHY MUST YOU WAIT, DARLING?"

in like that. But I did n't wait — not a minute.
And I did n't apologize, or say "Excuse me,"
or any of those things that I suppose I ought to
have done. I just started right in and began to
talk. And I talked hard and fast, and lots of it.

I don't know now what I said, but I know I
asked him what he meant by saying such an awful lie to my mother, when he'd just said the same
thing, exactly 'most, to Theresa, and he'd hugged
her and kissed her, and everything. I'd *seen* him.
And —

But I did n't get a chance to say half I wanted
to. I was going on to tell him what I thought of
him; but Mother gasped out, "Marie! *Marie!
Stop!*"

And then I stopped. I had to, of course. Then
she said that would do, and I might go to my
room. And I went. And that 's all I know about
it, except that she came up, after a little, and said
for me not to talk any more about it, to her, or
to any one else; and to please try to forget it.

I tried to tell her what I'd seen, and what I'd
heard that wicked, deep-dyed villain say; but
she would n't let me. She shook her head, and
said, "Hush, hush, dear"; and that no good
could come of talking of it, and she wanted me to
forget it. She was very sweet and very gentle,
and she smiled; but there were stern corners to
her mouth, even when the smile was there. And

I guess she told him what was what. Anyhow, I know they had quite a talk before she came up to me, for I was watching at the window for him to go; and when he did go he looked very red and cross, and he stalked away with a never-will-I-darken-this-door-again kind of a step, just as far as I could see him.

I don't know, of course, what will happen next, nor whether he'll ever come back for Theresa; but I should n't think even *she* would want him, after this, if she found out.

And now where's *my* love story coming in, I should like to know?

Two days after Christmas.

Another wonderful thing has happened. I've had a letter from Father — from *Father* — a *letter* — ME!

It came this morning. Mother brought it in to me. She looked queer — a little. There were two red spots in her cheeks, and her eyes were very bright.

"I think you have a letter here from — your father," she said, handing it out.

She hesitated before the "your father" just as she always does. And 't is n't hardly ever that she mentions his name, anyway. But when she does, she always stops a funny little minute before it, just as she did to-day.

And perhaps I'd better say right here, before I forget it, that Mother has been different, some way, ever since that time when the violinist proposed. I don't think she *cares* really — about the violinist, I mean — but she's just sort of upset over it. I heard her talking to Aunt Hattie one day about it, and she said:

"To think such a thing could happen — to *me!* And when for a minute I was really hesitating and thinking that maybe I *would* take him. Oh, Hattie!"

And Aunt Hattie put her lips together with her most I-told-you-so air, and said:

"It was, indeed, a narrow escape, Madge; and it ought to show you the worth of a real man. There's Mr. Easterbrook, now —"

But Mother wouldn't even listen then. She pooh-poohed and tossed her head, and said, "Mr. Easterbrook, indeed!" and put her hands to her ears, laughing, but in earnest just the same, and ran out of the room.

And she doesn't go so much with Mr. Easterbrook as she did. Oh, she goes with him some, but not enough to make it a bit interesting — for this novel, I mean — nor with any of the others, either. In fact, I'm afraid there isn't much chance now of Mother's having a love story to make this book right. Only the other day I heard her tell Grandfather and Aunt Hattie that *all* men were a delusion and a snare. Oh, she laughed as she said it. But she was in earnest, just the same. I could see that. And she does n't seem to care much for any of the different men that come to see her. She seems to ever so much rather stay with me. In fact, she stays with me a lot these days — almost all the time I'm out of school, indeed. And she talks with me — oh, she talks with me about lots of things. (I love to have her talk with me. You know there's a lot of difference between talking *with* folks and *to* folks. Now, Father always talks *to* folks.)

One day it was about getting married that Mother talked with me, and I said I was so glad that when you did n't like being married, or got tired of your husband, you could get *un*married, just as she did, and go back home and be just the same as you were before.

But Mother did n't like that, at all. She said no, no, and that I must n't talk like that, and that you *could n't* go back and be the same. And that she'd found it out. That she used to think you could. But you could n't. She said it was like what she read once, that you could n't really be the same any more than you could put the dress you were wearing back on the shelf in the store, and expect it to turn back into a fine long web of cloth all folded up nice and tidy, as it was in the first place. And, of course, you could n't do

that — after the cloth was all cut up into a
dress!

She said more things, too; and after Father's
letter came she said still more. Oh, and I have n't
told yet about the letter, have I? Well, I will now.

As I said at first, Mother brought it in and
handed it over to me, saying she guessed it was
from Father. And I could see she was wondering
what could be in it. But I guess she was n't wondering any more than *I* was, only I was gladder
to get it than she was, I suppose. Anyhow, when
she saw *how* glad I was, and how I jumped for
the letter, she drew back, and looked somehow
as if she'd been hurt, and said:

"I did not know, Marie, that a letter from —
your father would mean so much to you."

I don't know what I did say to that. I guess I
did n't say anything. I'd already begun to read
the letter, and I was in such a hurry to find out
what he'd said.

I'll copy it here. It was n't long. It was like
this:

My dear Mary:

Some way Christmas has made me think of you. I
wish I had sent you some gift. Yet I have not the
slightest idea what would please you. To tell the
truth, I tried to find something — but had to give it
up.

I am wondering if you had a good time, and what
you did. After all, I'm pretty sure you did have a

good time, for you are Marie now. You see I have not forgotten how tired you got of being — Mary. Well, well, I do not know as I can blame you.

And now that I have asked what you did for Christmas, I suspect it is no more than a fair turn-about to tell you·what I did. I suppose I had a very good time. Your Aunt Jane says I did. I heard her telling one of the neighbors that last night. She said she left no stone unturned to give me a good time. So, of course, I must have had a good time.

She had a very fine dinner, and she invited Mrs. Darling and Miss Snow and Miss Sanborn to eat it with us. She said she did n't want me to feel lonesome. But you can feel real lonesome in a crowd sometimes. Did you know that, Mary?

But I left them to their chatter after dinner and went out to the observatory. I think I must have fallen asleep on the couch there, for it was quite dark when I awoke. But I did n't mind that, for there were some observations I wanted to take. It was a beautifully clear night, so I stayed there till nearly morning.

How about it? I suppose Marie plays the piano every day now, does n't she? The piano here has n't been touched since you went away. Oh, yes, it was touched once. Your aunt played hymns on it for a missionary meeting.

Well, what did you do Christmas? Suppose you write and tell

Your

FATHER

I'd been reading the letter out loud, and when I got through Mother was pacing up and down the room. For a minute she did n't say anything;

then she whirled 'round suddenly and faced me,
and said, just as if something inside of her was
making her say it:

"I notice there is no mention of your mother
in that letter, Marie. I suppose — your father
has quite forgotten that there is such a person
in the world as — I."

But I told her no, oh, no, and that I was sure
he remembered her, for he used to ask me questions often about what she did, and the violinist
and all.

"The violinist!" cried Mother, whirling around
on me again. (She'd begun to walk up and down
once more.) "You don't mean to say you ever
told your father about *him!*"

"Oh, no, not everything," I explained, trying
to show how patient I was, so she would be patient, too. (But it did n't work.) "I could n't tell
him everything because everything had n't happened then. But I told about his being here, and
about the others, too; but, of course, I said I did
n't know which you'd take, and —"

"You told him you did n't know *which I'd
take!*" gasped Mother.

Just like that she interrupted, and she looked
so shocked. And she did n't look much better
when I explained very carefully what I did say,
even though I assured her over and over again
that Father was interested, very much interested.

When I said that, she just muttered, "Interested, indeed!" under her breath. Then she began to walk again, up and down, up and down. Then, all of a sudden, she flung herself on the couch and began to cry and sob as if her heart would break. And when I tried to comfort her, I only seemed to make it worse, for she threw her arms around me and cried:

"Oh, my darling, my darling, don't you see how dreadful it is, how dreadful it is?"

And then is when she began to talk some more about being married, and *un*married as we were. She held me close again and began to sob and cry.

"Oh, my darling, don't you see how dreadful it all is — how unnatural it is for us to live — this way? And for you — you poor child! — what could be worse for you? And here I am, jealous — jealous of your own father, for fear you'll love him better than you do me!

"Oh, I know I ought not to say all this to you — I know I ought not to. But I can't — help it. I want you! I want you every minute; but I have to give you up — six whole months of every year I have to give you up to him. And he's your father, Marie. And he's a good man. I know he's a good man. I know it all the better now since I've seen — other men. And I ought to tell you to love him. But I'm so afraid — you'll love him

better than you do me, and want to leave — me.
And I can't give you up! I can't give you up!"

Then I tried to tell her, of course, that she
would n't have to give me up, and that I loved
her a whole lot better than I did Father. But even
that did n't comfort her, 'cause she said I *ought*
to love *him*. That he was lonesome and needed
me. He needed me just as much as she needed
me, and maybe more. And then she went on again
about how unnatural and awful it was to live the
way we were living. And she called herself a
wicked woman that she'd ever allowed things
to get to such a pass. And she said if she could
only have her life to live over again she'd do so
differently — oh, so differently.

Then she began to cry again, and I could n't
do a thing with her; and of course, that worked
me all up and I began to cry.

She stopped then, right off short, and wiped
her eyes fiercely with her wet ball of a handkerchief. And she asked what was she thinking of,
and did n't she know any better than to talk like
this to me. Then she said, come, we'd go for a
ride.

And we did.

And all the rest of that day Mother was so gay
and lively you'd think she did n't know how to
cry.

Now, was n't that funny?

Of course, I shall answer Father's letter right away, but I have n't the faintest idea *what* to say.

One week later.

I answered it — Father's letter, I mean — yesterday, and it's gone now. But I had an awful time over it. I just did n't know what in the world to say. I'd start out all right, and I'd think I was going to get along beautifully. Then, all of a sudden, it would come over me, what I was doing — *writing a letter to my father!* And I could imagine just how he'd look when he got it, all stern and dignified, sitting in his chair in the library, and opening the letter *just so* with his paper-cutter; and I'd imagine his eyes looking down and reading what I wrote. And when I thought of that, my pen just would n't go. The idea of *my* writing anything my father would want to read!

And so I'd try to think of things that I could write — big things — big things that would interest big men: about the President, and our-country-'t is-of-thee, and the state of the weather and the crops. And so I'd begin:

"Dear Father: I take my pen in hand to inform you that — "

Then I'd stop and think and think, and chew my pen-handle. Then I'd put down *something*. But it was awful, and I knew it was awful. So I'd have to tear it up and begin again.

Three times I did that; then I began to cry. It did seem as if I never could write that letter. Once I thought of asking Mother what to say, and getting her to help me. Then I remembered how she cried and took on and said things when the letter came, and talked about how dreadful and unnatural it all was, and how she was jealous for fear I'd love Father better than I did her. And I was afraid she'd do it again, and so I did n't like to ask her. And so I did n't do it.

Then, after a time, I got out his letter and read it again. And all of a sudden I felt all warm and happy, just as I did when I first got it; and some way I was back with him in the observatory and he was telling me all about the stars. And I forgot all about being afraid of him, and about the crops and the President and my-country-'t is-of-thee. And I just remembered that he'd asked me to tell him what I did on Christmas Day; and I knew right off that that would be easy. Why, just the easiest thing in the world! And so I got out a fresh sheet of paper and dipped my pen in the ink and began again.

And this time I did n't have a bit of trouble. I told him all about the tree I had Christmas Eve, and the presents, and the little colored lights, and the fun we had singing and playing games. And then how, on Christmas morning, there was a lovely new snow on the ground, and Mr. Easter-

brook came with a perfectly lovely sleigh and
two horses to take Mother and me to ride, and
what a splendid time we had, and how lovely
Mother looked with her red cheeks and bright
eyes, and how, when we got home, Mr. Easterbrook said we looked more like sisters than
mother and daughter, and was n't that nice of him.
Of course, I told a little more about Mr. Easterbrook, too, so Father 'd know who he was — a new
friend of Mother's that I 'd never known till I came
back this time, and how he was very rich and a
most estimable man. That Aunt Hattie said so.

Then I told him that in the afternoon another
gentleman came and took us to a perfectly beautiful concert. And I finished up by telling about
the Christmas party in the evening, and how
lovely the house looked, and Mother, and that
they said I looked nice, too.

And that was all. And when I had got it done,
I saw that I had written a long letter, a great
long letter. And I was almost afraid it was too
long, till I remembered that Father had asked me
for it; he had *asked* me to tell him all about what
I did on Christmas Day.

So I sent it off.

March.

Yes, I know it 's been quite a while, but there
has n't been a thing to say — nothing new or

exciting, I mean. There's just school, and the usual things; only Mr. Easterbrook does n't come any more. (Of course, the violinist has n't come since that day he proposed.) I don't know whether Mr. Easterbrook proposed or not. I only know that all of a sudden he stopped coming. I don't know the reason.

I don't overhear so much as I used to, anyway. Not but that I'm in the library window-seat just the same; but 'most everybody that comes in looks there right off, now; and, of course, when they see me they don't hardly ever go on with what they are saying. So it just naturally follows that I don't overhear things as I used to.

Not that there's much to hear, though. Really, there just is n't anything going on, and things are n't half so lively as they used to be when Mr. Easterbrook was here, and all the rest. They've all stopped coming, now, 'most. I've about given up ever having a love story of Mother's to put in.

And mine, too. Here I am fifteen next month, going on sixteen. (Why, that brook and river met long ago!) But Mother is getting to be almost as bad as Aunt Jane was about my receiving proper attentions from young men. Oh, she lets me go to places, a little, with the boys at school; but I always have to be chaperoned. And whenever are they going to have a chance to say anything really *thrilling* with Mother or Aunt Hattie

right at my elbow? Echo answers never! So I've
about given up *that's* amounting to anything,
either.

Of course, there's Father left, and of course,
when I go back to Andersonville this summer,
there may be something doing there. But I
doubt it.

I forgot to say I have n't heard from Father
again. I answered his Christmas letter, as I said,
and wrote just as nice as I knew how, and told
him all he asked me to. But he never answered,
nor wrote again. I am disappointed, I'll own up.
I thought he would write. I think Mother did,
too. She's asked me ever so many times if I
had n't heard from him again. And she always
looks so sort of funny when I say no — sort of
glad and sorry together, all in one.

But, then, Mother's queer in lots of ways now.
For instance: One week ago she gave me a perfectly lovely box of chocolates — a whole two-
pound box all at once; and I've never had more
than a half-pound at once before. But just as I
was thinking how for once I was going to have a
real feast, and all I wanted to eat — what do you
think she told me? She said I could have three
pieces, and only three pieces a day; and not one
little tiny one more. And when I asked her why
she gave me such a big box for, then, if that was
all I could have, she said it was to teach me self-

discipline. That self-discipline was one of the most wonderful things in the world. That if she'd only been taught it when she was a girl, her life would have been very, very different. And so she was giving me a great big box of chocolates for my very own, just so as to teach me to deny myself and take only three pieces every day.

Three pieces! — and all that whole big box of them just making my mouth water all the while; and all just to teach me that horrid old self-discipline! Why, you'd think it was Aunt Jane doing it instead of Mother!

One week later.

It's come — Father's letter. It came last night. Oh, it was short, and it didn't say anything about what *I* wrote. But I was proud of it, just the same. I just guess I was! There wasn't much in it but just that I might stay till the school closed in June, and then come. But *he wrote it.* He didn't get Aunt Jane to write to Mother, as he did before. And then, besides, he must have forgotten his stars long enough to think of me a *little* — for he remembered about the school, and that I couldn't go there in Andersonville, and so he said I had better stay here till it finished.

And I was so glad to stay! It made me very happy — that letter. It made Mother happy, too. She liked it, and she thought it was very, very kind of Father to be willing to give me up almost three whole months of his six, so I could go to school here. And she said so. She said once to Aunt Hattie that she was almost tempted to write and thank him. But Aunt Hattie said, "Pooh," and it was no more than he ought to do, and that *she* would n't be seen writing to a man who so carefully avoided writing to *her*. So Mother did n't do it, I guess.

But I wrote. I had to write three letters, though, before I got one that Mother said would do to send. The first one sounded so *glad* I was staying that Mother said she was afraid he would feel hurt, and that would be too bad —when he'd been so kind. And the second one sounded as if I was so *sorry* not to go to Andersonville the first of April that Mother said that would never do in the world. He'd think I did n't *want* to stay in Boston. But the third letter I managed to make just glad enough to stay, and just sorry enough not to go. So that Mother said it was all right. And I sent it. You see I *asked* Mother to help me about this letter. I knew she would n't cry and moan about being jealous this time. And she did n't. She was real excited and happy over it.

April.

Well, the last chocolate drop went yesterday. There were just seventy-six pieces in that two-pound box. I counted them that first day. Of course, they were fine and dandy, and I just loved them; but the trouble is, for the last week I've been eating such snippy little pieces. You see, every day, without thinking, I'd just naturally pick out the biggest pieces. So you can imagine what they got down to toward the last — mostly chocolate almonds.

As for the self-discipline — I don't see as I feel any more disciplined than I did before, and I *know* I want chocolates just as much as ever. And I said so to Mother.

But Mother *is* queer. Honestly she is. And I can't help wondering — is she getting to be like Aunt Jane?

Now, listen to this:

Last week I had to have a new party dress, and we found a perfect darling of a pink silk, all gold beads, and gold slippers to match. And I knew I'd look perfectly divine in it; and once Mother would have got it for me. But not this time. She got a horrid white muslin with dots in it, and a blue silk sash, suitable for a child — for any child.

Of course, I was disappointed, and I suppose I did show it — some. In fact, I'm afraid I showed it a whole lot. Mother didn't say anything *then;* but on the way home in the car she put her arm around me and said:

"I'm sorry about the pink dress, dear. I knew you wanted it. But it was not suitable at all for you — not until you're older, dear."

She stopped a minute, then went on with another little hug:

"Mother will have to look out that her little daughter is n't getting to be vain, and too fond of dress."

I knew then, of course, that it was just some more of that self-discipline business.

But Mother never used to say anything about self-discipline.

Is she getting to be like Aunt Jane?

One week later.

She is.

I *know* she is now.

I'm learning to cook — *to cook!* And it's Mother that says I must. She told Aunt Hattie — I heard her — that she thought every girl should know how to cook and to keep house; and that if she had learned those things when she was a girl, her life would have been quite different, she was sure.

Of course, I'm not learning in Aunt Hattie's kitchen. Aunt Hattie's got a new cook, and she's worse than Olga used to be — about not wanting folks messing around, I mean. So Aunt Hattie said right off that we could n't do it there. I am learning at a Domestic Science School, and Mother is going with me. I did n't mind so much when she said she'd go, too. And, really, it is quite a lot of fun — really it is. But it *is* queer — Mother and I going to school together to learn how to make bread and cake and boil potatoes! And, of course, Aunt Hattie laughs at us. But I don't mind. And Mother does n't, either. But, oh, how Aunt Jane would love it, if she only knew!

May.

Something is the matter with Mother, certainly. She's acting queerer and queerer, and she *is* getting to be like Aunt Jane. Why, only this morning she hushed me up from laughing so loud, and stopped my romping up and down the stairs with Lester. She said it was noisy and unladylike — and only just a little while ago she just loved to have me laugh and play and be happy! And when I said so to her this morning, she said, yes, yes, of course, and she wanted me to be happy now, only she wished to remind me that very soon I was going back to my father in Andersonville, and that I ought to begin now to learn to be more quiet, so as not to trouble him when I got there.

Now, what do you think of that?

And another thing. What *do* you suppose I am

learning about *now?* You'd never guess. Stars.
Yes, *stars!* And that is for Father, too.

Mother came into my room one day with a
book of Grandfather's under her arm. She said
it was a very wonderful work on astronomy, and
she was sure I would find it interesting. She said
she was going to read it aloud to me an hour a
day. And then, when I got to Andersonville and
Father talked to me, I'd *know* something. And
he'd be pleased.

She said she thought we owed it to Father,
after he'd been so good and kind as to let me
stay here almost three whole months of his six,
so I could keep on with my school. And that she
was very sure this would please him and make
him happy.

And so, for 'most a week now, Mother has
read to me an hour a day out of that astronomy
book. Then we talk about it. And it *is* interesting. Mother says it is, too. She says she wishes
she'd known something about astronomy when
she was a girl; that she's sure it would have
made things a whole lot easier and happier all
around, when she married Father; for then she
would have known something about something
he was interested in. She said she couldn't help
that now, of course; but she could see that *I*
knew something about such things. And that
was why she was reading to me now. Then she

said again that she thought we owed it to Father,
when he'd been so good to let me stay.

It seems so funny to hear her talk such a lot
about Father as she does, when before she never
used to mention him — only to say how afraid
she was that I would love him better than I did
her, and to make me say over and over again
that I did n't. And I said so one day to her — I
mean, I said I thought it was funny, the way
she talked now.

She colored up and bit her lip, and gave a
queer little laugh. Then she grew very sober and
grave, and said:

"I know, dear. Perhaps I am talking more
than I used to. But, you see, I've been thinking
quite a lot, and I — I've learned some things.
And now, since your father has been so kind and
generous in giving you up to me so much of
his time, I — I've grown ashamed; and I'm
trying to make you forget what I said — about
your loving me more than him. That was n't
right, dear. Mother was wrong. She should n't
try to influence you against your father. He is a
good man; and there are none too many good
men in the world — No, no, I won't say that,"
she broke off.

But she'd already said it, and, of course, I
knew she was thinking of the violinist. I'm no
child.

She went on more after that, quite a lot more. And she said again that I must love Father and try to please him in every way; and she cried a little and talked a lot about how hard it was in my position, and that she was afraid she'd only been making it harder, through her selfishness, and I must forgive her, and try to forget it. And she was very sure she'd do better now. And she said that, after all, life wasn't in just being happy yourself. It was in how much happiness you could give to others.

Oh, it was lovely! And I cried, and she cried some more, and we kissed each other, and I promised. And after she went away I felt all upraised and holy, like you do when you've been to a beautiful church service with soft music and colored windows, and everybody kneeling. And I felt as if I'd never be naughty or thoughtless again. And that I'd never mind being Mary now. Why, I'd be glad to be Mary half the time, and even more — for Father.

But, alas!

Listen. Would you believe it? Just that same evening Mother stopped me again laughing too loud and making too much noise playing with Lester; and I felt real cross. I just boiled inside of me, and said I hated Mary, and that Mother *was* getting to be just like Aunt Jane. And yet, just that morning —

Oh, if only that hushed, stained-window-soft-music feeling *would* last!

June.

Well, once more school is done, my trunk is all packed, and I'm ready to go to Andersonville. I leave to-morrow morning. But not as I left last year. Oh, no. It is very, very different. Why, this year I'm really *going* as Mary. Honestly, Mother has turned me into Mary *before I go.* Now, what do you think of that? And if I've got to be Mary there and Mary here, too, when can I ever be *Marie?* Oh, I know I *said* I'd be willing to be Mary half, and maybe more than half, the time. But when it comes to really *being* Mary out of turn extra time, that is quite another thing.

And I am Mary.

Listen:

I've learned to cook. That's Mary.

I've been studying astronomy. That's Mary.

I've learned to walk quietly, speak softly, laugh not too loudly, and be a lady at all times. That's Mary.

And now, to add to all this, Mother has had me *dress* like Mary. Yes, she began two weeks ago. She came into my room one morning and said she wanted to look over my dresses and things; and I could see, by the way she frowned and bit her lip and tapped her foot on the floor, that she was n't suited. And I was glad; for, of course, I always like to have new things. So I was pleased when she said:

"I think, my dear, that on Saturday we'll have to go in town shopping. Quite a number of these things will not do at all."

And I was so happy! Visions of new dresses and hats and shoes rose before me, and even the pink beaded silk came into my mind — though I did n't really have much hopes of that.

Well, we went shopping on Saturday, but — did we get the pink silk? We did not. We did get — you'd never guess what. We got two new gingham dresses, very plain and homely, and a pair of horrid, thick low shoes. Why, I could have cried! I did 'most cry as I exclaimed:

"Why, Mother, those are *Mary* things!"

"Of course, they're Mary things," answered Mother, cheerfully — the kind of cheerfulness that says: "I'm being good and you ought to be." Then she went on. "That's what I meant to buy — Mary things, as you call them. Are n't you going to be Mary just next week? Of course, you are! And did n't you tell me last year, as soon as you got there, Miss Anderson objected to your clothing and bought new for you? Well, I am trying to see that she does not have to do that this year."

And then she bought me a brown serge suit and a hat so tiresomely sensible that even Aunt Jane will love them, I know. And to-morrow I've got to put them on to go in.

Do you wonder that I say I am Mary already?

CHAPTER VII

When I am Neither One

ANDERSONVILLE.

Well, I came last night. I had on the brown suit and the sensible hat, and every turn of the wheels all day had been singing: "Mary, Mary, now you're Mary!" Why, Mother even *called* me Mary when she said good-bye. She came to the junction with me just as she had before, and put me on the other train.

"Now, remember, dear, you're to try very hard to be a joy and a comfort to your father — just the little Mary that he wants you to be. Remember, he has been very kind to let you stay with me so long."

She cried when she kissed me just as she did before; but she did n't tell me this time to be sure and not love Father better than I did her. I noticed that. But, of course, I did n't say anything, though I might have told her easily that I knew nothing could ever make me love *him* better than I did *her*.

But I honestly tried, as long as I was dressed like Mary, to feel like Mary; and I made up my mind that I would *be* Mary, too, just as well as I knew how to be, so that even Aunt Jane could n't find any fault with me. And I'd try to please Father, and make him not mind my being there, even if I could n't make him love me. And as I got to thinking of it, I was *glad* that I had on the Mary things, so I would n't have to make any change. Then I could show Aunt Jane that I was really going to be Mary, right along from the start, when she met me at the station. And I would show Father, too, if he was at home. And I could n't help hoping he *would* be home this time, and not off to look at any old stars or eclipses.

When we got to Andersonville, and the train rolled into the station, I 'most forgot, for a minute, and ran down the aisle, so as to get out quick. I was so excited! But right away I thought of Aunt Jane and that she might see me; so I slowed down to a walk, and I let quite a lot of other folks get ahead of me, as I was sure Mary ought to. You see, I was determined to be a good little Mary from the very start, so that even Aunt Jane could n't find a word of fault — not even with my actions. I knew she could n't with my clothes!

Well, I stepped down from the cars and looked over to where the carriages were to find John and Aunt Jane. But they were n't there. There was n't even the carriage there; and I can remember now just how my heart sort of felt sick inside of me when I thought that even Aunt Jane had forgotten, and that there was n't anybody to meet me.

There was a beautiful big green automobile there, and I thought how I wished *that* had come to meet me; and I was just wondering what I should do, when all of a sudden somebody spoke my name. And who do you think it was? You'd never guess it in a month. It was *Father*. Yes, FATHER!

Why, I could have hugged him, I was so glad. But of course I did n't, right before all those people. But he was so tall and handsome and splendid, and I felt so proud to be walking along the platform with him and letting folks see that he'd come to meet me! But I could n't say anything — not anything, the way I wanted to; and all I could do was to stammer out:

"Why, where's Aunt Jane?"

And that's just the thing I did n't *want* to say; and I knew it the minute I'd said it. Why, it sounded as if I missed Aunt Jane, and wanted *her* instead of *him*, when all the time I was so pleased and excited to see him that I could hardly speak.

I don't know whether Father liked it, or minded it. I could n't tell by his face. He just kind of smiled, and looked queer, and said that Aunt Jane — er — could n't come. Then *I* felt sorry; for I saw, of course, that that was why *he* had come; not because he wanted to, but because Aunt Jane could n't, so he had to. And I could have cried, all the while he was fixing it up about my trunk.

He turned then and led the way straight over to where the carriages were, and the next minute there was John touching his cap to me; only it was a brand-new John looking too sweet for anything in a chauffeur's cap and uniform. And, what do you think? He was helping me into that beautiful big green car before I knew it.

"Why, Father, Father!" I cried. "You don't mean — " I just could n't finish; but he finished for me.

"It is ours — yes. Do you like it?"

"Like it!" I guess he did n't need to have me say any more. But I did say more. I just raved and raved over that car until Father's eyes crinkled all up in little smile wrinkles, and he said:

"I'm glad. I hoped you'd like it."

"I guess I do like it!" I cried. Then I went on to tell him how I thought it was the prettiest one I ever saw, and 'way ahead of even Mr. Easterbrook's.

"And, pray, who is Mr. Easterbrook?" asked Father then. "The violinist, perhaps — eh?"

Now, was n't it funny he should have remembered that there was a violinist? But, of course, I told him no, it was n't the violinist. It was another one that took Mother to ride, the one I told him about in the Christmas letter; and he was very rich, and had two perfectly beautiful cars; and I was going on to tell more — how he did n't take Mother now — but I did n't get a chance, for Father interrupted, and said, "Yes, yes, to be sure." And he *showed* he was n't interested, for all the little smile wrinkles were gone, and he looked stern and dignified, more like he used to. And he went on to say that, as we had almost reached home, he had better explain right away that Aunt Jane was no longer living there; that his cousin from the West, Mrs. Whitney, was keeping house for him now. She was a very nice lady, and he hoped I would like her. And I might call her "Cousin Grace."

And before I could even draw breath to ask any questions, we were home; and a real pretty lady, with a light-blue dress on, was helping me out of the car, and kissing me as she did so.

Now, do you wonder that I have been rubbing my eyes and wondering if I was really I, and if this was Andersonville? Even now I 'm not sure but it 's a dream, and I shall wake up and find I 've gone to sleep on the cars, and that the train is just drawing into the station, and that John and the horses, and Aunt Jane in her I-don't-

care-how-it-looks black dress are there to meet
me.

One week later.

It is n't a dream. It's all really, truly true —
everything: Father coming to meet me, the lovely
automobile, and the pretty lady in the light-blue
dress, who kissed me. And when I went downstairs the next morning I found out it was real,
'specially the pretty lady; for she kissed me again,
and said she hoped I'd be happy there. And she
never said one word about dusting one hour and
studying one hour and weeding one hour. (Of
course, she could n't say anything about my
clothes, for I was already in a Mary blue-ging-
ham dress.) She just told me to amuse myself
any way I liked, and said, if I wanted to, I might
run over to see some of the girls, but not to make
any plans for the afternoon, for she was going to
take me to ride.

Now, what do you think of that? Go to see the
girls in the morning, and take a ride — an automobile ride! — in the afternoon. *In Andersonville!* Why, I could n't believe my ears. Of course,
I was wild and crazy with delight — but it was
all so different. Why, I began to think almost
that I was Marie, and not Mary at all.

And it's been that way the whole week through.
I've had a beautiful time. I've been so excited!

And Mother is excited, too. Of course, I wrote her and told her all about it right away. And she wrote right back and wanted to know everything — everything I could tell her; all the little things. And she was so interested in Cousin Grace, and wanted to know all about her; said *she* never heard of her before, and was she Father's own cousin, and how old was she, and was she pretty, and was Father around the house more now, and did I see a lot of him? She thought from something I said that I did.

I've just been writing her again, and I could tell her more now, of course, than I could in that first letter. I've been here a whole week, and, of course, I know more about things, and have done more.

I told her that Cousin Grace was n't really Father's cousin at all, so it was n't any wonder she had n't ever heard of her. She was the wife of Father's third cousin who went to South America six years ago and caught the fever and died there. So this Mrs. Whitney is n't really any relation of his at all. But he'd always known her, even before she married his cousin; and so, when her husband died, and she did n't have any home, he asked her to come here.

I don't know why Aunt Jane went away, but she's been gone 'most four months now, they say here. Nellie told me. Nellie is the maid — I mean hired girl — here now. (I *will* keep forgetting that I'm Mary now and must use the Mary words here.)

I told Mother that she (Cousin Grace) was quite old, but not so old as Aunt Jane. (I asked Nellie, and Nellie said she guessed she was thirty-five, but she did n't look a day over twenty-five.) And she *is* pretty, and everybody loves her. I think even Father likes to have her around better than he did his own sister Jane, for he sometimes stays around quite a lot now — after meals, and in the evening, I mean. And that's what I told Mother. Oh, of course, he still likes his stars the best of anything, but not quite as well as he used to, maybe — not to give *all* his time to them.

I have n't anything especial to write. I'm just having a beautiful time. Of course, I miss Mother, but I know I'm going to have her again in just September — I forgot to say that Father is going to let me go back to school again this year ahead of his time, just as he did last year.

So you see, really, I'm here only a little bit of a while, as it is now, and it's no wonder I keep forgetting I am Mary.

I have n't got anything new for the love part of my story. I *am* sorry about that. But there just is n't anything, so I'm afraid the book never will be a love story, anyway.

Of course, I'm not with Mother now, so I don't

know whether there's anything there, or not; but I don't think there will be. And as for Father — I've pretty nearly given him up. Anyhow, there never used to be any signs of hope for me there. As for myself — well, I've about given that up, too. I don't believe they're going to give me any chance to have anybody till I'm real old — probably not till I'm twenty-one or two. And I can't wait all that time to finish this book.

One week later.

Things are awfully funny here this time. I wonder if it's all Cousin Grace that makes it so. Anyhow, she's just as different as different can be from Aunt Jane. And *things* are different, everywhere.

Why, I forget half the time that I'm Mary. Honestly, I do. I try to be Mary. I try to move quietly, speak gently, and laugh softly, just as Mother told me to. But before I know it I'm acting natural again — just like Marie, you know.

And I believe it *is* Cousin Grace. She never looks at you in Aunt Jane's I'm-amazed-at-you way. And she laughs herself a lot, and sings and plays, too — real pretty lively things; not just hymn tunes. And the house is different. There are four geraniums in the dining-room window, and the parlor is open every day. The wax flowers are there, but the hair wreath and the coffin plate are gone. Cousin Grace does n't dress like Aunt Jane, either. She wears pretty white and blue dresses, and her hair is curly and fluffy.

And so I think all this is why I keep forgetting to be Mary. But, of course, I understand that Father expects me to be Mary, and so I try to remember — only I can't. Why, I could n't even show him how much I knew about the stars. I tried to the other night. I went out to the observatory where he was, and asked him questions about the stars. I tried to seem interested, and was going to tell him how I'd been studying about them, but he just laughed kind of funny, and said not to bother my pretty head about such things, but to come in and play to him on the piano.

So, of course, I did. And he sat and listened to three whole pieces. Now, was n't that funny?

Two weeks later.

I understand it all now —everything: why the house is different, and Father, and everything. And it *is* Cousin Grace, and it *is* a love story.

Father is in love with her.

Now I guess I shall have something for this book!

It seems funny now that I did n't think of it at first. But I did n't — not until I heard Nellie and her beau talking about it. Nellie said she was n't the only one in the house that was going to get married. And when he asked her what she meant, she said it was Dr. Anderson and Mrs. Whitney. That anybody could see it that was n't as blind as a bat.

My, but was n't I excited? I just guess I was. And, of course, I saw then that I had been blind as a bat. But I began to open my eyes after that, and watch — not disagreeably, you know, but just glad and interested, and on account of the book.

And I saw:

That father stayed in the house a lot more than he used to.

That he talked more.

That he never thundered — I mean spoke stern and uncompromising to Cousin Grace the way he used to to Aunt Jane.

That he smiled more.

That he was n't so absent-minded at meals and other times, but seemed to know we were there — Cousin Grace and I.

That he actually asked Cousin Grace and me to play for him several times.

That he went with us to the Sunday-School picnic. (I never saw Father at a picnic before, and I don't believe he ever saw himself at one.)

That — oh, I don't know, but a whole lot of

little things that I can't remember; but they
were all unmistakable, very unmistakable. And
I wondered, when I saw it all, that I *had* been as
blind as a bat before.

Of course, I was glad — glad he's going to
marry her, I mean. I was glad for everybody;
for Father and Cousin Grace, for they would be
happy, of course, and he would n't be lonesome
any more. And I was glad for Mother because I
knew she'd be glad that he'd at last found the
good, kind woman to make a home for him.
And, of course, I was glad for myself, for I'd
much rather have Cousin Grace here than Aunt
Jane, and I knew she'd make the best new
mother of any of them. And last, but not least,
I'm glad for the book, because now I've got a
love story sure. That is, I'm pretty sure. Of
course, it may not be so; but I think it is.

When I wrote Mother I told her all about it —
the signs and symptoms, I mean, and how different and thawed-out Father was; and I asked
if she did n't think it was so, too. But she did n't
answer that part. She did n't write much, anyway. It was an awfully snippy letter; but she
said she had a headache and did n't feel at all
well. So that was the reason, probably, why she
did n't say more — about Father's love affair,
I mean. She only said she was glad, she was sure,
if Father had found an estimable woman to make

a home for him, and she hoped they'd be happy.
Then she went on talking about something else.
And she did n't write much more, anyway, about
anything.

August.

Well, of all the topsy-turvy worlds, this is the
topsy-turviest, I am sure. What *do* they want me
to do, and which do they want me to be? Oh, I
wish I was just a plain Susie or Bessie, and not a
cross-current and a contradiction, with a father
that wants me to be one thing and a mother
that wants me to be another! It was bad enough
before, when Father wanted me to be Mary, and
Mother wanted me to be Marie. But now —

Well, to begin at the beginning.

It's all over — the love story, I mean, and I
know now why it's been so hard for me to remember to be Mary and why everything is
different, and all.

They don't want me to be Mary.

They want me to be Marie.

And now I don't know what to think. If
Mother's going to want me to be Mary, and
Father's going to want me to be Marie, how
am I going to know what anybody wants, ever?
Besides, it was getting to be such a beautiful
love story — Father and Cousin Grace. And
now —

But let me tell you what happened.

It was last night. We were on the piazza, Father, Cousin Grace, and I. And I was thinking how perfectly lovely it was that Father *was* there, and that he was getting to be so nice and folksy, and how I *did* hope it would last, even after he'd married her, and not have any of that incompatibility stuff come into it. Well, just then she got up and went into the house for something — Cousin Grace, I mean — and all of a sudden I determined to tell Father how glad I was, about him and Cousin Grace; and how I hoped it would last — having him out there with us, and all that. And I told him.

I don't remember what I said exactly. But I know I hurried on and said it fast, so as to get in all I could before he interrupted; for he had interrupted right at the first with an exclamation; and I knew he was going to say more right away, just as soon as he got a chance. And I didn't want him to get a chance till I'd said what *I* wanted to. But I hadn't anywhere near said what I wanted to when he did stop me. Why, he almost jumped out of his chair.

"Mary!" he gasped. "What in the world are you talking about?"

"Why, Father, I was telling you," I explained. And I tried to be so cool and calm that it would make him calm and cool, too. (But it didn't calm him or cool him one bit.) "It's about when you're married, and — "

"Married!" he interrupted again. (They never let *me* interrupt like that!)

"To Cousin Grace — yes. But, Father, you — you *are* going to marry Cousin Grace, are n't you?" I cried — and I did 'most cry, for I saw by his face that he was not.

"That is not my present intention," he said. His lips came together hard, and he looked over his shoulder to see if Cousin Grace was coming back.

"But you're going to *sometime*," I begged him.

"I do not expect to." Again he looked over his shoulder to see if she was coming. I looked, too, and we both saw through the window that she had gone into the library and lighted up and was sitting at the table reading.

I fell back in my chair, and I know I looked grieved and hurt and disappointed, as I almost sobbed:

"Oh, Father, and when I *thought* you were going to!"

"There, there, child!" He spoke, stern and almost cross now. "This absurd, nonsensical idea has gone quite far enough. Let us think no more about it."

"It is n't absurd and nonsensical!" I cried. And I could hardly say the words, I was choking up so. "Everybody said you were going to, and I wrote Mother so; and — "

"You wrote that to your mother?" He did jump from his chair this time.

"Yes; and she was glad."

"Oh, she was!" He sat down sort of limp-like and queer.

"Yes. She said she was glad you'd found an estimable woman to make a home for you."

"Oh, she did." He said this, too, in that queer, funny, quiet kind of way.

"Yes." I spoke, decided and firm. I'd begun to think, all of a sudden, that maybe he did n't appreciate Mother as much as she did him; and I determined right then and there to make him, if I could. When I remembered all the lovely things she'd said about him —

"Father," I began; and I spoke this time, even more decided and firm. "I don't believe you appreciate Mother."

"Eh? What?"

He made *me* jump this time, he turned around with such a jerk, and spoke so sharply. But in spite of the jump I still held on to my subject, firm and decided.

"I say I don't believe you appreciate my mother. You acted right now as if you did n't believe she meant it when I told you she was glad you had found an estimable woman to make a home for you. But she did mean it. I know, because she said it before, once, last year, that she hoped you *would* find one."

"Oh, she did." He sat back in his chair again, sort of limp-like. But I could n't tell yet, from his face, whether I'd convinced him or not. So I went on.

"Yes, and that is n't all. There's another reason why I know Mother always has — has your best interest at heart. She — she tried to make me over into Mary before I came, so as to please you."

"She did *what?*" Once more he made me jump, he turned so suddenly, and spoke with such a short, sharp snap.

But in spite of the jump I went right on, just as I had before, firm and decided. I told him everything — all about the cooking lessons, and the astronomy book we read an hour every day, and the pink silk dress I could n't have, and even about the box of chocolates and the self-discipline. And how she said if she'd had self-discipline when she was a girl, her life would have been very different. And I told him about how she began to hush me up from laughing too loud, or making any kind of noise, because I was soon to be Mary, and she wanted me to get used to it, so I would n't trouble him when I got here.

I talked very fast and hurriedly. I was afraid

he'd interrrupt, and I wanted to get in all I could before he did. But he didn't interrupt at all. I couldn't see how he was taking it, though — what I said — for after the very first he sat back in his chair and shaded his eyes with his hand; and he sat like that all the time I was talking. He did not even stir until I said how at the last she bought me the homely shoes and the plain dark suit so I could go as Mary, and be Mary when Aunt Jane first saw me get off the train.

When I said that, he dropped his hand and turned around and stared at me. And there was such a funny look in his eyes.

"I *thought* you didn't look the same!" he cried; "not so white and airy and — and — I can't explain it, but you looked different. And yet, I didn't think it could be so, for I knew you looked just as you did when you came, and that no one had asked you to — to put on Mary's things this year."

He sort of smiled when he said that; then he got up and began to walk up and down the piazza, muttering: "So you *came* as Mary, you *came* as Mary." Then, after a minute, he gave a funny little laugh and sat down.

Mrs. Small came up the front walk then to see Cousin Grace, and Father told her to go right into the library where Cousin Grace was. So we were left alone again, after a minute.

It was 'most dark on the piazza, but I could see Father's face in the light from the window; and it looked — well, I'd never seen it look like that before. It was as if something that had been on it for years had dropped off and left it clear where before it had been blurred and indistinct. No, that does n't exactly describe it either. I *can't* describe it. But I'll go on and say what he said.

After Mrs. Small had gone into the house, and he saw that she was sitting down with Cousin Grace in the library, he turned to me and said:

"And so you came as Mary?"

I said yes, I did.

"Well, I — I got ready for Marie."

But then I did n't quite understand, not even when I looked at him, and saw the old understanding twinkle in his eyes.

"You mean — you thought I was coming as Marie, of course," I said then.

"Yes," he nodded.

"But I came as Mary."

"I see now that you did." He drew in his breath with a queer little catch to it; then he got up and walked up and down the piazza again. (Why do old folks always walk up and down the room like that when they're thinking hard about something? Father always does; and Mother does lots of times, too.) But it was n't but a minute this time before Father came and sat down.

"Well, Mary," he began; and his voice sounded odd, with a little shake in it. "You've told me your story, so I suppose I may as well tell you mine — now. You see, I not only got ready for Marie, but I had planned to keep her Marie, and not let her be Mary — at all."

And then he told me. He told me how he'd never forgotten that day in the parlor when I cried (and made a wet spot on the arm of the sofa — *I* never forgot that!), and he saw then how hard it was for me to live here, with him so absorbed in his work and Aunt Jane so stern in her black dress. And he said I put it very vividly when I talked about being Marie in Boston, and Mary here, and he saw just how it was. And so he thought and thought about it all winter, and wondered what he could do. And after a time it came to him — he'd let me be Marie here; that is, he'd try to make it so I could be Marie. And he was just wondering how he was going to get Aunt Jane to help him when she was sent for and asked to go to an old friend who was sick. And he told her to go, by all means to go. Then he got Cousin Grace to come here. He said he knew Cousin Grace, and he was very sure she would know how to help him to let me stay Marie. So he talked it over with her — how they would let me laugh, and sing and play the piano all I wanted to, and wear the clothes I brought with

me, and be just as near as I could be the way I was
in Boston.

"And to think, after all my preparation for
Marie, you should *be* Mary already, when you
came," he finished.

"Yes. Was n't it funny?" I laughed. "All the
time *you* were getting ready for Marie, Mother
was getting me ready to be Mary. It *was* funny!"
And it did seem funny to me then.

But Father was not laughing. He had sat back
in his chair, and had covered his eyes with his
hand again, as if he was thinking and thinking,
just as hard as he could. And I suppose it did
seem queer to him, that he should be trying to
make me Marie, and all the while Mother was
trying to make me Mary. And it seemed so to me,
as I began to think it over. It was n't funny at
all, any longer.

"And so your mother — did that," Father muttered; and there was the queer little catch in his
breath again.

He did n't say any more, not a single word.
And after a minute he got up and went into the
house. But he did n't go into the library where
Mrs. Small and Cousin Grace were talking. He
went straight upstairs to his own room and shut
the door. I heard it. And he was still there when
I went up to bed afterwards.

Well, I guess he does n't feel any worse than I

do. I thought at first it was funny, a good joke
— his trying to have me Marie while Mother
was making me over into Mary. But I see now
that it is n't. It 's awful. Why, how am I going to
know at all who to be — now? Before, I used to
know just when to be Mary, and when to be
Marie — Mary with Father, Marie with Mother.
Now I don't know at all. Why, they can't even
seem to agree on that! I suppose it 's just some
more of that incompatibility business showing
up even when they are apart. And poor me —
I have to suffer for it. I 'm beginning to see that
the child does suffer — I mean the child of unlikes.

Now, look at me right now — about my clothes,
for instance. (Of course clothes are a little thing,
you may think; but I don't think anything's little that 's always with you like clothes are!) Well,
here all summer, and even before I came, I 've
been wearing stuffy gingham and clumpy shoes
to please Father. And Father is n't pleased at
all. He wanted me to wear the Marie things.

And there you are.

How do you suppose Mother 's going to feel
when I tell her that after all her pains Father
did n't like it at all. He wanted me to be Marie.
It 's a shame, after all the pains she took. But I
won't write it to her, anyway. Maybe I won't
have to tell her, unless she *asks* me.

But *I* know it. And, pray, what am I to do? Of course, I can *act* like Marie here all right, if that is what folks want. (I guess I have been doing it a good deal of the time, anyway, for I kept forgetting that I was Mary.) But I can't *wear* Marie, for I have n't a single Marie thing here. They're all Mary. That's all I brought.

Oh, dear suz me! Why could n't Father and Mother have been just the common live-happy-ever-after kind, or else found out before they married that they were unlikes?

September.

Well, vacation is over, and I go back to Boston to-morrow. It's been very nice and I've had a good time, in spite of being so mixed up as to whether I was Mary or Marie. It was n't so bad as I was afraid it would be. Very soon after Father and I had that talk on the piazza, Cousin Grace took me down to the store and bought me two new white dresses, and the dearest little pair of shoes I ever saw. She said Father wanted me to have them.

And that's all — every single word that's been said about that Mary-and-Marie business. And even that did n't really *say* anything — not by name. And Cousin Grace never mentioned it again. And Father never mentioned it at all. Not a word.

But he's been queer. He's been awfully queer.
Some days he's been just as he was when I first
came this time — real talky and folksy, and as if
he liked to be with us. Then for whole days at a
time he'd be more as he used to — stern, and
stirring his coffee when there is n't any coffee
there; and staying all the evening and half the
night out in his observatory.

Some days he's talked a lot with me — asked
me questions just as he used to, all about what I
did in Boston, and Mother, and the people that
came there to see her, and everything. And he
spoke of the violinist again, and, of course, this
time I told him all about him, and that he did n't
come any more, nor Mr. Easterbrook, either; and
Father was *so* interested! Why, it seemed sometimes as if he just could n't hear enough about
things. Then, all of a sudden, at times, he'd get
right up in the middle of something I was saying
and act as if he was just waiting for me to finish
my sentence so he could go. And he did go, just
as soon as I *had* finished my sentence. And after
that, maybe, he would n't hardly speak to me
again for a whole day.

And so that's why I say he's been so queer
since that night on the piazza. But most of the
time he's been lovely, perfectly lovely. And so
has Cousin Grace. And I've had a beautiful time.

But I do wish they *would* marry — Father and

Cousin Grace, I mean. And I'm not talking now entirely for the sake of the book. It's for their sakes — especially for Father's sake. I've been thinking what Mother used to say about him, when she was talking about my being Mary — how he was lonely, and needed a good, kind woman to make a home for him. And while I've been thinking of it, I've been watching him; and I think he does need a good, kind woman to make a home for him. I'd be *willing* to have a new mother for his sake!

Oh, yes, I know he's got Cousin Grace, but he may not have her always. Maybe she'll be sent for same as Aunt Jane was. *Then* what's he going to do, I should like to know?

CHAPTER VIII

WHICH IS THE REAL LOVE STORY

BOSTON. *Four days later.*

Well, here I am again in Boston. Mother and the rest met me at the station, and everybody seemed glad to see me, just as they did before. And I was glad to see them. But I did n't feel anywhere near so excited, and sort of crazy, as I did last year. I tried to, but I could n't. I don't know why. Maybe it was because I'd been Marie all summer, anyway, so I was n't so crazy to be Marie now, not needing any rest from being Mary. Maybe it was 'cause I sort of hated to leave Father.

And I did hate to leave him, especially when I found he hated to have me leave him. And he did. He told me so at the junction. You see, our train was late, and we had to wait for it; and there was where he told me.

He had come all the way down there with me, just as he had before. But he had n't acted the same at all. He did n't fidget this time, nor walk over to look at maps and time-tables, nor flip out his watch every other minute with such a bored air that everybody knew he was seeing me off just as a duty. And he did n't ask if I was warmly clad, and had I left anything, either. He just sat and talked to me, and he asked me had I been a little happier there with him this year than last; and he said he hoped I had.

And I told him, of course, I had; that it had been perfectly beautiful there, even if there had been such a mix-up of him getting ready for Marie, and Mother sending Mary. And he laughed and looked queer — sort of half glad and half sorry; and said he should n't worry about that. Then the train came, and we got on and rode down to the junction. And there, while we were waiting for the other train, he told me how sorry he was to have me go.

He said I would never know how he missed me after I went last year. He said you never knew how you missed things — and people — till they were gone. And I wondered if, by the way he said it, he was n't thinking of Mother more than he was of me, and of her going long ago. And he looked so sort of sad and sorry and noble and handsome, sitting there beside me, that suddenly I 'most wanted to cry. And I told him I *did* love him, I loved him dearly, and I had loved to be with him this summer, and that I 'd stay his whole six months with him next year if he wanted me to.

He shook his head at that; but he did look happy and pleased, and said I 'd never know how glad he was that I 'd said that, and that he should prize it very highly — the love of his little daughter. He said you never knew how to prize love, either, till you'd lost it; and he said he'd learned his lesson, and learned it well. I knew then, of course, that he was thinking of Mother and the long ago. And I felt so sorry for him.

"But I'll stay — I'll stay the whole six months next year!" I cried again.

But again he shook his head.

"No, no, my dear; I thank you, and I'd love to have you; but it is much better for you that you stay in Boston through the school year, and I want you to do it. It'll just make the three months I do have you all the dearer, because of the long nine months that I do not," he went on very cheerfully and briskly; "and don't look so solemn and long-faced. You're not to blame — for this wretched situation."

The train came then, and he put me on board, and he kissed me again — but I was expecting it this time, of course. Then I whizzed off, and he was left standing all alone on the platform. And I felt so sorry for him; and all the way down to Boston I kept thinking of him — what he said, and how he looked, and how fine and splendid and any-woman-would-be-proud-of-him he was as he stood on the platform waving good-bye.

And so I guess I was still thinking of him and being sorry for him when I got to Boston. That's why I could n't be so crazy and hilariously glad when the folks met me, I suspect. Some way, all of a sudden, I found myself wishing *he* could be there, too.

Of course, I knew that that was bad and wicked and unkind to Mother, and she'd feel so grieved not to have me satisfied with her. And I would n't have told her of it for the world. So I tried just as hard as I could to forget him — on account of Mother, so as to be loyal to her. And I did 'most forget him by the time I'd got home. But it all came back again a little later when we were unpacking my trunk.

You see, Mother found the two new white dresses, and the dear little shoes. I knew then, of course, that she'd have to know all — I mean, how she had n't pleased Father, even after all her pains trying to have me go as Mary.

"Why, Marie, what in the world is this?" she demanded, holding up one of the new dresses.

I could have cried.

I suppose she saw by my face how awfully I felt 'cause she'd found it. And, of course, she saw something was the matter; and she thought it was —

Well, the first thing *I* knew she was looking at me in her very sternest, sorriest way, and saying:

"Oh, Marie, how could you? I'm ashamed of

you! Could n't you wear the Mary dresses one
little three months to please your father?"

I did cry, then. After all I'd been through, to
have her accuse *me* of getting those dresses! Well,
I just could n't stand it. And I told her so as well
as I could, only I was crying so by now that I
could hardly speak. I told her how it was hard
enough to be Mary part of the time, and Marie
part of the time, when I *knew* what they wanted
me to be. But when she tried to have me Mary
while he wanted me Marie, and he tried to have
me Marie while she wanted me Mary — I did
not know what they wanted; and I wished I had
never been born unless I could have been born
a plain Susie or Bessie, or Annabelle, and not a
Mary Marie that was all mixed up till I did n't
know what I was.

And then I cried some more.

Mother dropped the dress then, and took me in
her arms over on the couch, and she said, "There,
there," and that I was tired and nervous, and all
wrought up, and to cry all I wanted to. And by
and by, when I was calmer I could tell Mother all
about it.

And I did.

I told her how hard I tried to be Mary all the
way up to Andersonville and after I got there;
and how then I found out, all of a sudden one
day, that father had got ready for *Marie*, and he

did n't want me to be Mary, and that was why he had got Cousin Grace and the automobile and the geraniums in the window, and, oh, everything that made it nice and comfy and homey. And then is when they bought me the new white dresses and the little white shoes. And I told Mother, of course, it was lovely to be Marie, and I liked it, only I knew *she* would feel bad to think, after all *her* pains to make me Mary, Father did n't want me Mary at all.

"I don't think you need to worry — about that," stammered Mother. And when I looked at her, her face was all flushed, and sort of queer, but not a bit angry. And she went on in the same odd little shaky voice: "But, tell me, why — why did — your father want you to be Marie and not Mary?"

And then I told her how he said he'd remembered what I'd said to him in the parlor that day — how tired I got being Mary, and how I'd put on Marie's things just to get a little vacation from her; and he said he'd never forgotten. And so when it came near time for me to come again, he determined to fix it so I would n't have to be Mary at all. And so that was why. And I told Mother it was all right, and of course I liked it; only it *did* mix me up awfully, not knowing which wanted me to be Mary now, and which Marie, when they were both telling me different from

what they ever had before. And that it was hard,
when you were trying just the best you knew how.

And I began to cry again.

And she said there, there, once more, and patted me on my shoulder, and told me I need n't
worry any more. And that *she* understood it, if I
did n't. In fact, she was beginning to understand
a lot of things that she'd never understood before. And she said it was very, very dear of Father
to do what he did, and that I need n't worry
about her being displeased at it. That she was
pleased, and that she believed he meant her to be.
And she said I need n't think any more whether
to be Mary or Marie; but to be just a good, loving
little daughter to both of them; and that was all
she asked, and she was very sure it was all Father
would ask, too.

I told her then how I thought he *did* care a little
about having me there, and that I knew he was
going to miss me. And I told her why — what
he'd said that morning in the junction — about
appreciating love, and not missing things or people until you did n't have them; and how he'd
learned his lesson, and all that.

And Mother grew all flushed and rosy again,
but she was pleased. I knew she was. And she
said some beautiful things about making other
people happy, instead of looking to ourselves all
the time, just as she had talked once, before I

went away. And I felt again that hushed, stained-window, soft-music, everybody-kneeling kind of a way; and I was so happy! And it lasted all the rest of that evening till I went to sleep.

And for the first time a beautiful idea came to me, when I thought how Mother was trying to please Father, and he was trying to please her. Would n't it be perfectly lovely and wonderful if Father and Mother should fall in love with each other all over again, and get married? I guess *then* this would be a love story all right, all right!

October.

Oh, how I wish that stained-window, everybody-kneeling feeling *would* last. But it never does. Just the next morning, when I woke up, it rained. And I did n't feel pleased a bit. Still I remembered what had happened the night before, and a real glow came over me at the beautiful idea I had gone to sleep with.

I wanted to tell Mother, and ask her if it could n't be, and would n't she let it be, if Father would. So, without waiting to dress me, I hurried across the hall to her room and told her all about it — my idea, and everything.

But she said, "Nonsense," and, "Hush, hush," when I asked her if she and Father could n't fall in love all over again and get married. And she said not to get silly notions into my head. And

she was n't a bit flushed and teary, as she had
been the night before, and she did n't talk at all
as she had then, either. And it's been that way
ever since. Things have gone along in just the
usual humdrum way, and she's never been the
same as she was that night I came.

Something — a little something — *did* happen
yesterday, though. There's going to be another
big astronomy meeting here in Boston this month,
just as there was when Father found Mother
years ago; and Grandfather brought home word
that Father was going to be one of the chief
speakers. And he told Mother he supposed she'd
go and hear him.

I could n't make out whether he was joking or
not. (I never can tell when Grandfather's joking.)
But Aunt Hattie took it right up in earnest, and
said, "Pooh, pooh," she guessed not. She could
see Madge going down to that hall to hear Dr.
Anderson speak!

And then a funny thing happened. I looked at
Mother, and I saw her head come up with a queer
little jerk.

"Well, yes, I am thinking of going," she said,
just as calm and cool as could be. "When does he
speak, Father?"

And when Aunt Hattie pooh-poohed some
more, and asked how *could* she do such a thing,
Mother answered:

"Because Charles Anderson is the father of my little girl, and I think she should hear him speak. Therefore, Hattie, I intend to take her."

And then she asked Grandfather again when Father was going to speak.

I'm so excited! Only think of seeing my father up on a big platform with a lot of big men, and hearing him speak! And he'll be the very smartest and handsomest one there, too. You see if he is n't!

Two weeks and one day later.

Oh, I've got a lot to write this time — I mean, a lot has happened. Still, I don't know as it's going to take so very long to tell it. Besides, I'm almost too excited to write, anyway. But I'm going to do the best I can to tell it, just as it happened.

Father's here — right here in Boston. I don't know when he came. But the first day of the meeting was day before yesterday, and he was here then. The paper said he was, and his picture was there, too. There were a lot of pictures, but his was away ahead of the others. It was the very best one on the page. (I told you it would be that way.)

Mother saw it first. That is, I think she did. She had the paper in her hand, looking at it, when I came into the room; but as soon as she saw me she laid it right down quick on the table. If she had n't been quite so quick about it, and if she had n't looked quite so queer when she did it, I would n't have thought anything at all. But when I went over to the table after she had gone, and saw the paper with Father's picture right on the first page — and the biggest picture there — I knew then, of course, what she'd been looking at.

I looked at it then, and I read what it said, too. It was lovely. Why, I had n't any idea Father was so big. I was prouder than ever of him. It told all about the stars and comets he'd discovered, and the books he'd written on astronomy, and how he was president of the college at Andersonville, and that he was going to give an address the next day. And I read it all — every word. And I made up my mind right there and then that I'd cut out that piece and save it.

But that night, when I went to the library cupboard to get the paper, I could n't do it, after all. Oh, the paper was there, but that page was gone. There was n't a bit of it left. Somebody had taken it right out. I never thought then of Mother. But I believe now that it *was* Mother, for —

But I must n't tell you that part now. Stories are just like meals. You have to eat them — I mean tell them in regular order, and not put the ice-cream in where the soup ought to be. So

I'm not going to tell yet why I suspect it was Mother that cut out that page of the paper with Father's picture in it.

Well, the next morning was Father's lecture, and I went with Mother. Of course Grandfather was there, too, but he was with the other astronomers, I guess. Anyhow, he did n't sit with us. And Aunt Hattie did n't go at all. So Mother and I were alone.

We sat back — a long ways back. I wanted to go up front, real far front — the front seat, if I could get it; and I told Mother so. But she said, "Mercy, no!" and shuddered, and went back two more rows from where she was, and got behind a big post.

I guess she was afraid Father would see us, but that's what *I* wanted. I wanted him to see us. I wanted him to be right in the middle of his lecture and look down and see right there before him his little girl Mary, and she that had been the wife of his bosom. Now *that* would have been what I called thrilling, real thrilling, especially if he jumped or grew red, or white, or stammered, or stopped short, or anything to show that he'd seen us — and cared.

I'd have loved that.

But we sat back where Mother wanted to, behind the post. And, of course, Father never saw us at all.

It was a lovely lecture. Oh, of course, I don't mean to say that I understood it. I did n't. But his voice was fine, and he looked just too grand for anything, with the light on his noble brow, and he used the loveliest big words that I ever heard. And folks clapped, and looked at each other, and nodded, and once or twice they laughed. And when he was all through they clapped again, harder than ever. And I was so proud of him I wanted to stand right up and holler, "He's my father! He's my father!" just as loud as I could. But, of course, I did n't. I just clapped like the rest; only I wished my hands were big like the man's next to me, so I could have made more noise.

Another man spoke then, a little (not near so good as Father), and then it was all over, and everybody got up to go; and I saw that a lot of folks were crowding down the aisle, and I looked and there was Father right in front of the platform shaking hands with folks.

I looked at Mother then. Her face was all pinky-white, and her eyes were shining. I guess she thought I spoke, for all of a sudden she shook her head and said:

"No, no, I could n't, I could n't! But *you* may, dear. Run along and speak to him; but don't stay. Remember, Mother is waiting, and come right back."

I knew then that it must have been just my eyes that spoke, for I *did* want to go down there and speak to Father. Oh, I did want to go! And I went then, of course.

He did n't see me at first. There was a long line of us, and a big fat man was doing a lot of talking to him so we could n't move at all, for a time. Then it came to when I was just three people away from him. And I was looking straight at him.

He saw me then. And, oh, how I did love the look that came to his face; it was so surprised and glad, and said, "Oh! *You!*" in such a perfectly lovely way that I choked all up and wanted to *cry*. (The idea! — cry when I was so *glad* to see him!)

I guess the two folks ahead of me did n't think they got much attention, and the next minute he had drawn me out of the line, and we were both talking at once, and telling each other how glad we were to see each other.

But he was looking for Mother — I know he was; for the next minute after he saw me, he looked right over my head at the woman back of me. And all the while he was talking with me, his eyes would look at me and then leap as swift as lightning first here, and then there, all over the hall. But he did n't see her. I knew he did n't see her, by the look on his face. And pretty quick I said I'd have to go. And then he said:

"Your mother — perhaps she did n't — *did* she come?" And his face grew all red and rosy as he asked the question.

And I said yes, and she was waiting, and that was why I had to go back right away.

And he said, "Yes, yes, to be sure," and, "good-bye." But he still held my hand tight, and his eyes were still roving all over the house. And I had to tell him again that I really had to go; and I had to pull real determined at my hand, before I could break away. And I don't believe I could have gone even then if some other folks had n't come up at that minute.

I went back to Mother then. The hall was almost empty, and she was n't anywhere in sight at all; but I found her just outside the door. I knew then why Father's face showed that he had n't found her. She was n't there to find. I suspect she had looked out for that.

Her face was still pinky-white, and her eyes were shining; and she wanted to know everything we had said — everything. So she found out, of course, that he had asked if she was there. But she did n't say anything herself, not anything. She did n't say anything, either, at the luncheon table, when Grandfather was talking with Aunt Hattie about the lecture, and telling some of the things Father had said.

Grandfather said it was an admirable address, scholarly and convincing, or something like that. And he said that he thought Dr. Anderson had improved greatly in looks and manner. And he looked straight at Mother when he said that; but still Mother never said a word.

In the afternoon I went to walk with one of the girls; and when I came in I could n't find Mother. She was n't anywhere downstairs, nor in her room, nor mine, nor anywhere else on that floor. Aunt Hattie said no, she was n't out, but that she was sure she did n't know where she was. She must be somewhere in the house.

I went upstairs then, another flight. There was n't anywhere else to go, and Mother must be *somewhere*, of course. And it seemed suddenly to me as if I'd just *got* to find her. I *wanted* her so.

And I found her.

In the little back room where Aunt Hattie keeps her trunks and moth-ball bags, Mother was on the floor in the corner crying. And when I exclaimed out and ran over to her, I found she was sitting beside an old trunk that was open; and across her lap was a perfectly lovely pale-blue satin dress all trimmed with silver lace that had grown black. And Mother was crying and crying as if her heart would break.

Of course, I tried and tried to stop her, and I begged her to tell me what was the matter. But I could n't do a thing, not a thing, not for a long time. Then I happened to say what a lovely dress, only what a pity it was that the lace was all black.

She gave a little choking cry then, and began to talk — little short sentences all choked up with sobs, so that I could hardly tell what she was talking about. Then, little by little, I began to understand.

She said yes, it was all black — tarnished; and that it was just like everything that she had had anything to do with — tarnished: her life and her marriage, and Father's life, and mine — everything was tarnished, just like that silver lace on that dress. And she had done it by her thoughtless selfishness and lack of self-discipline.

And when I tried and tried to tell her no, it was n't, and that I did n't feel tarnished a bit, and that she was n't, nor Father either, she only cried all the more, and shook her head and began again, all choked up.

She said this little dress was the one she wore at the big reception where she first met Father. It was a beautiful blue then, all shining and spotless, and the silver lace glistened like frost in the sunlight. And she was so proud and happy when Father — and he was fine and splendid

and handsome then, too, she said — singled her
out, and just could n't seem to stay away from
her a minute all the evening. And then four days
later he asked her to marry him; and she was
still more proud and happy.

And she said their married life, when they
started out, was just like that beautiful dress, all
shining and spotless and perfect; but that it
was n't two months before a little bit of tarnish
appeared, and then another and another.

She said she was selfish and willful and exacting, and wanted Father all to herself; and she did
n't stop to think that he had his work to do, and
his place to make in the world; and that all of
living, to him, was n't just in being married to
her, and attending to her every whim. She said
she could see it all now, but that she could n't
then, she was too young, and undisciplined, and
she'd never been denied a thing in the world she
wanted. As she said that, right before my eyes
rose that box of chocolates she made me eat one
at a time; but, of course, I did n't say anything!
Besides, Mother hurried right on talking.

She said things went on worse and worse —
and it was all her fault. She grew sour and cross
and disagreeable. She could see now that she
did. But she did not realize at all then what
she was doing. She was just thinking of herself —
always herself; her rights, her wrongs, her hurt

feelings, her wants and wishes. She never once thought that *he* had rights and wrongs and hurt feelings, maybe.

And so the tarnish kept growing more and more. She said there was nothing like selfishness to tarnish the beautiful fabric of married life. (Isn't that a lovely sentence? I said that over and over to myself so as to be sure and remember it, so I could get it into this story. I thought it was beautiful.)

She said a lot more — oh, ever so much more; but I can't remember it all. (I lost some while I was saying that sentence over and over, so as to remember it.) I know that she went on to say that by and by the tarnish began to dim the brightness of my life, too; and that was the worst of all, she said — that innocent children should suffer, and their young lives be spoiled by the kind of living I'd had to have, with this wretched makeshift of a divided home. She began to cry again then, and begged me to forgive her, and I cried and tried to tell her I didn't mind it; but, of course, I'm older now, and I know I do mind it, though I'm trying just as hard as I can not to be Mary when I ought to be Marie, or Marie when I ought to be Mary. Only I get all mixed up so, lately, and I said so, and I guess I cried some more.

Mother jumped up then, and said, "Tut, tut,"

what was she thinking of to talk like this when
it could n't do a bit of good, but only made
matters worse. And she said that only went to
prove how she was still keeping on tarnishing my
happiness and bringing tears to my bright eyes,
when certainly nothing of the whole wretched
business was my fault.

She thrust the dress back into the trunk then,
and shut the lid. Then she took me downstairs
and bathed my eyes and face with cold water,
and hers, too. And she began to talk and laugh
and tell stories, and be gayer and jollier than I 'd
seen her for ever so long. And she was that way
at dinner, too, until Grandfather happened to
mention the reception to-morrow night, and ask
if she was going.

She flushed up red then, oh, so red! and said,
" Certainly not." Then she added quick, with a
funny little drawing-in of her breath, that she
should let Marie go, though, with her Aunt
Hattie.

There was an awful fuss then. Aunt Hattie
raised her eyebrows and threw up her hands,
and said:

"That child — in the evening! Why, Madge,
are you crazy?"

And Mother said no, she was n't crazy at all;
but it was the only chance Father would have to
see me, and she did n't feel that she had any

right to deprive him of that privilege, and she did n't think it would do me any harm to be out this once late in the evening. And she intended to let me go.

Aunt Hattie still did n't approve, and she said more, quite a lot more; but Grandfather spoke up and took my part, and said that, in his opinion, Madge was right, quite right, and that it was no more than fair that the man should have a chance to talk with his own child for a little while, and that he would be very glad to take me himself and look after me, if Aunt Hattie did not care to take the trouble.

Aunt Hattie bridled up at that, and said that that was n't the case at all; that she'd be very glad to look after me; and if Mother had quite made up her mind that she wanted me to go, they'd call the matter settled.

And Mother said she had, and so it was settled. And I'm going. I'm to wear my new white dress with the pink rosebud trimming, and I'm so excited I can hardly wait till to-morrow night. But — oh, if only Mother would go, too!

Two days later.

Well, *now* I guess something's doing all right! And my hand is shaking so I can hardly write — it wants to get ahead so fast and *tell*. But I'm going to keep it sternly back and tell it just as it happened, and not begin at the ice-cream instead of the soup.

Very well, then. I went last night with Grandfather and Aunt Hattie to the reception; and Mother said I looked very sweet, and any-father-ought-to-be-proud-of me in my new dress. Grandfather patted me, put on his glasses, and said, "Well, well, bless my soul! Is this our little Mary Marie?" And even Aunt Hattie said if I acted as well as I looked I'd do very well. Then Mother kissed me and ran upstairs *quick*. But I saw the tears in her eyes, and I knew why she hurried so.

At the reception I saw Father right away, but he did n't see me for a long time. He stood in a corner, and lots of folks came up and spoke to him and shook hands; and he bowed and smiled — but in between, when there was n't anybody noticing, he looked so tired and bored. After a time he stirred and changed his position, and I think he was hunting for a chance to get away, when all of a sudden his eyes, roving around the room, lighted on me.

My! but just did n't I love the way he came through that crowd, straight toward me, without paying one bit of attention to the folks that tried to stop him on the way. And when he got to me, he looked so glad to see me, only there was the same quick searching with his eyes, beyond and around me, as if he was looking for somebody else, just as he had done the morning of the lecture. And I knew it was Mother, of course. So I said:

"No, she did n't come."

"So I see," he answered. And there was such a hurt, sorry look away back in his eyes. But right away he smiled, and said: "But *you* came! I 've got *you*."

Then he began to talk and tell stories, just as if I was a young lady to be entertained. And he took me over to where they had things to eat, and just heaped my plate with chicken patties and sandwiches and olives and pink-and-white frosted cakes and ice-cream (not all at once, of course, but in order). And I had a perfectly beautiful time. And Father seemed to like it pretty well. But after a while he grew sober again, and his eyes began to rove all around the room.

He took me to a little seat in the corner then, and we sat down and began to talk — only Father did n't talk much. He just listened to what I said, and his eyes grew deeper and darker and sadder, and they did n't rove around so much, after a time, but just stared fixedly at nothing, away out across the room. By and by he stirred and drew a long sigh, and said, almost under his breath:

"It was just such another night as this."

And of course, I asked what was — and then I knew, almost before he had told me.

"That I first saw your mother, my dear."

"Oh, yes, I know!" I cried, eager to tell him that I *did* know. "And she must have looked lovely in that perfectly beautiful blue silk dress all silver lace."

He turned and stared at me.

"How did *you* know that?" he demanded.

"I saw it."

"You *saw* it!"

"Yesterday, yes — the dress," I nodded.

"But how *could* you?" he asked, frowning, and looking so surprised. "Why, that dress must be — seventeen years old, or more."

I nodded again, and I suppose I did look pleased: it's such fun to have a secret, you know, and watch folks guess and wonder. And I kept him guessing and wondering for quite a while. Then, of course, I told him that it was upstairs in Grandfather's trunk-room; that Mother had got it out, and I saw it.

"But, what — was your mother doing with that dress?" he asked then, looking even more puzzled and mystified.

And then suddenly I thought and remembered that Mother was crying. And, of course, she would n't want Father to know she was crying over it — that dress she had worn when he first met her long ago! (I don't think women ever want men to know such things, do you? I know I should n't!) So I did n't tell. I just kind of tossed it off, and mumbled something about her looking it over; and I was going to say something else, but I saw that Father was n't listening. He had begun to talk again, softly, as if to himself.

"I suppose to-night, seeing you, and all this, brought it back to me so vividly." Then he turned and looked at me. "You are very like your mother to-night, dear."

"I suppose I am, maybe, when I'm Marie," I nodded.

He laughed with his lips, but his eyes did n't laugh one bit as he said:

"What a quaint little fancy of yours that is, child — as if you were two in one."

"But I am two in one," I declared. "That's why I'm a cross-current and a contradiction, you know," I explained.

I thought he'd understand. But he did n't. I supposed, of course, he knew what a cross-current and a contradiction was. But he turned again and stared at me.

"A — *what?*" he demanded.

"A cross-current and a contradiction," I explained once more. "Children of unlikes, you

know. Nurse Sarah told me that long ago. Did n't
you ever hear that — that a child of unlikes
was a cross-current and a contradiction?"

"Well, no — I — had n't," answered Father,
in a queer, half-smothered voice. He half started
from his seat. I think he was going to walk up
and down, same as he usually does. But in a
minute he saw he could n't, of course, with all
those people around there. So he sat back again
in his chair. For a minute he just frowned and
stared at nothing; then he spoke again, as if half
to himself.

"I suppose, Mary, we were — unlikes, your
mother and I. That's just what we were; though
I never thought of it before, in just that way."

He waited, then went on, still half to himself,
his eyes on the dancers:

"She loved things like this — music, laughter,
gayety. I abhorred them. I remember how bored
I was that night here — till I saw her."

"And did you fall in love with her right away?"
I just could n't help asking that question. Oh, I
do so adore love stories!

A queer little smile came to Father's lips.

"Well, yes, I think I did, Mary. There'd been
dozens and dozens of young ladies that had
flitted by in their airy frocks — and I never
looked twice at them. I never looked twice at
your mother, for that matter, Mary." (A funny

little twinkle came into Father's eyes. I *love* him with that twinkle!) "I just looked at her once — and then kept on looking till it seemed as if I just could n't take my eyes off her. And after a little her glance met mine — and the whole throng melted away, and there was n't another soul in the room but just us two. Then she looked away, and the throng came back. But I still looked at her."

"Was she so awfully pretty, Father?" I could feel the little thrills tingling all over me. *Now* I was getting a love story!

"She was, my dear. She was very lovely. But it was n't just that — it was a joyous something that I could not describe. It was as if she were a bird, poised for flight. I know it now for what it was — the very incarnation of the spirit of youth. And she *was* young. Why, Mary, she was not so many years older than you yourself, now."

I nodded, and I guess I sighed.

"I know — where the brook and river meet," I said; "only they won't let *me* have any lovers at all."

"Eh? What?" Father had turned and was looking at me so funny. "Well, no, I should say not," he said then. "You are n't sixteen yet. And your mother — I suspect *she* was too young. If she had n't been quite so young — "

He stopped, and stared again straight ahead

at the dancers — without seeing one of them, I knew. Then he drew a great deep sigh that seemed to come from the very bottom of his boots.

"But it was my fault, my fault, every bit of it," he muttered, still staring straight ahead. "If I had n't been so thoughtless — As if I could imprison that bright spirit of youth in a great dull cage of conventionality, and not expect it to bruise its wings by fluttering against the bars!"

I thought that was perfectly beautiful — that sentence. I said it right over to myself two or three times so I would n't forget how to write it down here. So I did n't quite hear the next things that Father said. But when I did notice, I found he was still talking — and it was about Mother, and him, and their marriage, and their first days at the old house. I knew it was that, even if he did mix it all up about the spirit of youth beating its wings against the bars. And over and over again he kept repeating that it was his fault, it was his fault; and if he could only live it over again he 'd do differently.

And right there and then it came to me that Mother said it was her fault, too; and that if only she could live it over again, *she'd* do differently. And here was Father saying the same thing. And all of a sudden I thought, well, why

can't they try it over again, if they both want
to, and if each says it was their — no, his, no,
hers — well, his and her fault. (How does the
thing go? I hate grammar!) But I mean, if she
says it's her fault, and he says it's his. That's
what I thought, anyway. And I determined
right then and there to give them the chance to
try again, if speaking would do it.

I looked up at Father. He was still talking
half under his breath, his eyes looking straight
ahead. He had forgotten all about me. That was
plain to be seen. If I'd been a cup of coffee without any coffee in it, he'd have been stirring me.
I know he would. He was like that.

"Father. *Father!*" I had to speak twice, before he heard me. "Do you really mean that you
would like to try again?" I asked.

"Eh? What?" And just the way he turned
and looked at me showed how many *miles* he'd
been away from me.

"Try it again, you know — what you said,"
I reminded him.

"Oh, that!" Such a funny look came to his
face, half ashamed, half vexed. "I'm afraid I
have been — talking, my dear."

"Yes, but would you?" I persisted.

He shook his head; then, with such an oh-
that-it-could-be! smile, he said:

"Of course; — we all wish that we could go

back and do it over again — differently. But we never can."

"I know; like the cloth that's been cut up into the dress," I nodded.

"Cloth? Dress?" frowned Father.

"Yes, that Mother told me about," I explained. Then I told him the story that Mother had told me — how you could n't go back and be unmarried, just as you were before, any more than you could put the cloth back on the shelf, all neatly folded in a great long web after it had been cut up into a dress.

"Did your mother say — that?" asked Father. His voice was husky, and his eyes were turned away, but they were not looking at the dancers. He was listening to me now. I knew that, and so I spoke quick, before he could get absent-minded again.

"Yes, but, Father, you can go back, in this case, and so can Mother, 'cause you both want to," I hurried on, almost choking in my anxiety to get it all out quickly. "And Mother said it was *her* fault. I heard her."

"*Her* fault!" I could see that Father did not quite understand, even yet.

"Yes, yes, just as you said it was yours — about all those things at the first, you know, when — when she was a spirit of youth beating against the bars."

Father turned square around and faced me.

"Mary, what are you talking about?" he asked then. And I'd have been scared of his voice if it had n't been for the great light that was shining in his eyes.

But I looked into his eyes, and was n't scared; and I told him everything, every single thing — all about how Mother had cried over the little blue dress that day in the trunk-room, and how she had shown the tarnished lace and said that *she* had tarnished the happiness of him and of herself and of me; and that it was all her fault; that she was thoughtless and willful and exacting and a spoiled child; and, oh, if she could only try it over again, how differently she would do! And there was a lot more. I told everything — everything I could remember. Some way, I did n't believe that Mother would mind *now*, after what Father had said. And I just knew she would n't mind if she could see the look in Father's eyes as I talked.

He did n't interrupt me — not long interruptions. He did speak out a quick little word now and then, at some of the parts; and once I know I saw him wipe a tear from his eyes. After that he put up his hand and sat with his eyes covered all the rest of the time I was talking. And he did n't take it down till I said:

"And so, Father, that's why I told you; 'cause

it seemed to me if *you* wanted to try again, and *she* wanted to try again, why can't you do it? Oh, Father, think how perfectly lovely 't would be if you did, and if it worked! Why, I would n't care whether I was Mary or Marie, or what I was. I'd have you and Mother both together, and, oh, how I should love it!"

It was just here that Father's arm came out and slipped around me in a great big hug.

"Bless your heart! But, Mary, my dear, how are we going to — to bring this about?" And he actually stammered and blushed, and he looked almost young with his eyes so shining and his lips so smiling. And then is when my second great idea came to me.

"Oh, Father!" I cried, "could n't you come courting her again — calls and flowers and candy, and all the rest? Oh, Father, could n't you? Why, Father, of course, you could!"

This last I added in my most persuasive voice, for I could see the "no" on his face even before he began to shake his head.

"I'm afraid not, my dear," he said then. "It would take more than a flower or a bonbon to — to win your mother back now, I fear."

"But you could try," I urged.

He shook his head again.

"She would n't see me — if I called, my dear," he answered.

He sighed as he said it, and I sighed, too. And for a minute I did n't say anything. Of course, if she would n't *see* him —

Then another idea came to me.

"But, Father, if she *would* see you — I mean, if you got a chance, you *would* tell her what you told me just now; about — about its being your fault, I mean, and the spirit of youth beating against the bars, and all that. You would, would n't you?"

He did n't say anything, not anything, for such a long time I thought he had n't heard me. Then, with a queer, quick drawing-in of his breath, he said:

"I think — little girl — if — if I ever got the chance I would say — a great deal more than I said to you to-night."

"Good!" I just crowed the word, and I think I clapped my hands, but right away I straightened up and was very fine and dignified, for I saw Aunt Hattie looking at me from across the room, as I said:

"Very good, then. You shall have the chance."

He turned and smiled a little, but he shook his head.

"Thank you, child; but I don't think you know quite what you're promising," he said.

"Yes, I do."

Then I told him my idea. At first he said no, and it could n't be, and he was very sure she would n't see him, even if he called. But I said she would if he would do exactly as I said. And I told him my plan. And after a time and quite a lot of talk, he said he would agree to it.

And this morning we did it.

At exactly ten o'clock he came up the steps of the house here, but he did n't ring the bell. I had told him not to do that, and I was on the watch for him. I knew that at ten o'clock Grandfather would be gone, Aunt Hattie probably downtown shopping, and Lester out with his governess. I was n't so sure of Mother, but I knew it was Saturday, and I believed I could manage somehow to keep her here with me, so that everything would be all right there.

And I did. I had a hard time, though. Seems as if she proposed everything to do this morning — shopping, and a walk, and a call on a girl I knew who was sick. But I said I did not feel like doing anything but just to stay at home and rest quietly with her. (Which was the truth — I *did n't* feel like doing *anything else!*) But that almost made matters worse than ever, for she said that was so totally unlike me that she was afraid I must be sick; and I had all I could do to keep her from calling a doctor.

But I did it; and at five minutes before ten she

THEN I TOLD HIM MY IDEA

was sitting quietly sewing in her own room. Then
I went downstairs to watch for Father.

He came just on the dot, and I let him in and
took him into the library. Then I went upstairs
and told Mother there was some one downstairs
who wanted to see her.

And she said, how funny, and was n't there any
name, and where was the maid. But I did n't
seem to hear. I had gone into my room in quite a
hurry, as if I had forgotten something I wanted
to do there. But, of course, I did n't do a thing —
except to make sure that she went downstairs to
the library.

They 're there now *together*. And he 's been here
a whole hour already. Seems as if he ought to say
something in that length of time!

After I was sure Mother was down, I took out
this, and began to write in it. And I 've been writing ever since. But, oh, I do so wonder what 's
going on down there. I 'm so excited over —

One week later.

At just that minute Mother came into the
room. I wish you could have seen her. My stars,
but she looked pretty! — with her shining eyes
and the lovely pink in her cheeks. And *young!*
Honestly, I believe she looked younger than I
did that minute.

She just came and put her arms around me

and kissed me; and I saw then that her eyes were all misty with tears. She did n't say a word, hardly, only that Father wanted to see me, and I was to go right down.

And I went.

I thought, of course, that she was coming too. But she did n't. And when I got down the stairs I found I was all alone; but I went right on into the library, and there was Father waiting for me.

He did n't say much, either, at first; but just like Mother he put his arms around me and kissed me, and held me there. Then, very soon, he began to talk; and, oh, he said such beautiful things — such tender, lovely, sacred things; too sacred even to write down here. Then he kissed me again and went away.

But he came back the next day, and he's been here some part of every day since. And, oh, what a wonderful week it has been!

They're going to be married. It's to-morrow. They'd have been married right away at the first, only they had to wait — something about licenses and a five-day notice, Mother said. Father fussed and fumed, and wanted to try for a special dispensation, or something; but Mother laughed, and said certainly not, and that she guessed it was just as well, for she positively *had* to have a few things; and he need n't think he could walk right in like that on a body and expect her to get married at a moment's notice. But she did n't mean it. I know she did n't; for when Father reproached her, she laughed softly, and called him an old goose, and said, yes, of course, she 'd have married him in two minutes if it had n't been for the five-day notice, no matter whether she ever had a new dress or not.

And that 's the way it is with them all the time. They 're too funny and lovely together for anything. (Aunt Hattie says they 're too silly for anything; but nobody minds Aunt Hattie.) They just can't seem to do enough for each other. Father was going next week to a place 'way on the other side of the world to view an eclipse of the moon, but he said right off he 'd give it up. But Mother said, "No, indeed," she guessed he *would n't* give it up; that he was going, and that she was going, too — a wedding trip; and that she was sure she did n't know a better place to go for a wedding trip than the moon! And Father was *so* pleased. And he said he 'd try not to pay all his attention to the stars this time; and Mother laughed and said, "Nonsense," and that she adored stars herself, and that he *must* pay attention to the stars. It was his business to. Then she looked very wise and got off something she 'd read in the astronomy book. And they both laughed, and looked over to me to see if I was noticing. And I was. And so then we all laughed.

And, as I said before, it is all perfectly lovely and wonderful.

So it's all settled, and they're going right away on this trip and call it a wedding trip. And, of course, Grandfather had to get off his joke about how he thought it was a pretty dangerous business; and to see that *this* honeymoon didn't go into an eclipse while they were watching the other one. But nobody minds Grandfather.

I'm to stay here and finish school. Then, in the spring, when Father and Mother come back, we are all to go to Andersonville and begin to live in the old house again.

Won't it be lovely? It just seems too good to be true. Why, I don't care a bit now whether I'm Mary or Marie. But, then, nobody else does, either. In fact, both of them call me the whole name now, Mary Marie. I don't think they ever *said* they would. They just began to do it. That's all.

Of course, anybody can see why: *now* each one is calling me the other one's name along with their own. That is, Mother is calling me Mary along with her pet Marie, and Father is calling me Marie along with his pet Mary.

Funny, isn't it?

But one thing is sure, anyway. How about this being a love story *now?* Oh, I'm so excited!

CHAPTER IX

WHICH IS THE TEST

ANDERSONVILLE. *Twelve years later*.

Twelve years — yes. And I'm twenty-eight years old. Pretty old, little Mary Marie of the long ago would think. And, well, perhaps to-day I feel just as old as she would put it.

I came up into the attic this morning to pack away some things I shall no longer need, now that I am going to leave Jerry. (Jerry is my husband.) And in the bottom of my little trunk I found this manuscript. I had forgotten that such a thing existed; but with its laboriously written pages before me, it all came back to me; and I began to read; here a sentence; there a paragraph; somewhere else a page. Then, with a little half laugh and half sob, I carried it to an old rocking-chair by the cobwebby dormer window, and settled myself to read it straight through.

And I have read it.

Poor little Mary Marie! Dear little Mary Marie! To meet you like this, to share with you your joys and sorrows, hopes and despairs, of those years long ago, is like sitting hand in hand on a sofa with a childhood's friend, each listening to

an eager "And do you remember?" falling con-
stantly from delighted lips that cannot seem to
talk half fast enough.

But you have taught me much, little Mary
Marie. I understand — oh, I understand so many
things so much better, now, since reading this
little story in your round childish hand. You
see, I had almost forgotten that I was a Mary
and a Marie — Jerry calls me Mollie — and I
had wondered what were those contending forces
within me. I know now. It is the Mary and the
Marie trying to settle their old, old quarrel.

It was almost dark when I had finished the
manuscript. The far corners of the attic were
peopled with fantastic shadows, and the spi-
ders in the window were swaying, lazy and full-
stomached, in the midst of the day's spoils of
gruesome wings and legs. I got up slowly, stiffly,
shivering a little. I felt suddenly old and worn
and ineffably weary. It is a long, long journey
back to our childhood — sometimes, even though
one may be only twenty-eight.

I looked down at the last page of the manuscript. It was written on the top sheet of a still
thick pad of paper, and my fingers fairly tingled
suddenly, to go on and cover those unused white
sheets — tell what happened next — tell the rest
of the story; not for the sake of the story — but
for my sake. It might help me. It might make

things clearer. It might help to justify myself in my own eyes. Not that I have any doubts, of course (about leaving Jerry, I mean), but that when I saw it in black and white I could be even more convinced that I was doing what was best for him and best for me.

So I brought the manuscript down to my own room, and this evening I have commenced to write. I can't finish it to-night, of course. But I have to-morrow, and still to-morrow. (I have so many to-morrows now! And what do they all amount to?) And so I'll just keep writing, as I have time, till I bring it to the end.

I'm sorry that it must be so sad and sorry an end. But there's no other way, of course. There can be but one ending, as I can see. I'm sorry. Mother'll be sorry, too. She does n't know yet. I hate to tell her. Nobody knows — not even Jerry himself — yet. They all think I'm just making a visit to Mother — and I am — till I write that letter to Jerry. And then —

I believe now that I'll wait till I've finished writing this. I'll feel better then. My mind will be clearer. I'll know more what to say. Just the effort of writing it down —

Of course, if Jerry and I had n't —

But this is no way to begin. Like the little Mary Marie of long ago I am in danger of starting my dinner with ice-cream instead of soup!

And so I must begin where I left off, of course. And that was at the wedding.

I remember that wedding as if it were yesterday. I can see now, with Mary Marie's manuscript before me, why it made so great an impression upon me. It was a very quiet wedding, of course — just the members of the family present. But I shall never forget the fine, sweet loveliness of Mother's face, nor the splendid strength and tenderness of Father's. And the way he drew her into his arms and kissed her, after it was all over — well, I remember distinctly that even Aunt Hattie choked up and had to turn her back to wipe her eyes.

They went away at once, first to New York for a day or two, then to Andersonville, to prepare for the real wedding trip to the other side of the world. I stayed in Boston at school; and because nothing of consequence happened all those weeks and months is the reason, I suspect, why the manuscript got tossed into the bottom of my little trunk and stayed there.

In the spring, when Father and Mother returned, and we all went back to Andersonville, there followed another long period of just happy girlhood, and I suspect I was too satisfied and happy to think of writing. After all, I've noticed it's when we're sad or troubled over something that we have that tingling to cover perfectly good white paper with "confessions" and "stories of my life." As witness right now what I'm doing.

And so it's not surprising, perhaps, that Mary Marie's manuscript still lay forgotten in the little old trunk after it was taken up to the attic. Mary Marie was happy.

And it *was* happy — that girlhood of mine, after we came back to Andersonville. I can see now, as I look back at it, that Father and Mother were doing everything in their power to blot out of my memory those unhappy years of my childhood. For that matter, they were also doing everything in their power to blot out of their *own* memories those same unhappy years. To me, as I look back at it, it seems that they must have succeeded wonderfully. They were very happy, I believe — Father and Mother.

Oh, it was not always easy — even I could see that. It took a lot of adjusting — a lot of rubbing off of square corners to keep the daily life running smoothly. But when two persons are determined that it shall run smoothly — when each is steadfastly looking to the *other's* happiness, not at his own — why, things just can't help smoothing out then. But it takes them both. One can't do it alone. Now, if Jerry would only —

But it is n't time to speak of Jerry yet.

I'll go back to my girlhood.

It was a trying period — it must have been — for Father and Mother, in spite of their great love for me, and their efforts to create for me a happiness that would erase the past from my mind. I realize it now. For, after all, I was just a girl — a young girl, like other girls; high-strung, nervous, thoughtless, full of my whims and fancies; and, in addition, with enough of my mother and enough of my father within me to make me veritably a cross-current and a contradiction, as I had said that I was in the opening sentence of my childish autobiography.

I had just passed my sixteenth birthday when we all came back to live in Andersonville. For the first few months I suspect that just the glory and the wonder and joy of living in the old home, with Father and Mother *happy together*, was enough to fill all my thoughts. Then, as school began in the fall, I came down to normal living again, and became a girl — just a growing girl in her teens.

How patient Mother was, and Father, too! I can see now how gently and tactfully they helped me over the stones and stumbling-blocks that strew the pathway of every sixteen-year-old girl who thinks, because she has turned down her dresses and turned up her hair, that she is grown up, and can do and think and talk as she pleases.

I well remember how hurt and grieved and

superior I was at Mother's insistence upon more frequent rubbers and warm coats, and fewer ice-cream sodas and chocolate bonbons. Why, surely I was old enough *now* to take care of myself! Was n't I ever to be allowed to have my own opinions and exercise my own judgment? It seemed not! Thus spoke superior sixteen.

As for clothes! — I remember distinctly the dreary November rainstorm of the morning I reproachfully accused Mother of wanting to make me back into a stupid little Mary, just because she so uncompromisingly disapproved of the beaded chains and bangles and jeweled combs and spangled party dresses that "every girl in school" was wearing. Why, the idea! Did she want me to dress like a little frump of a country girl? It seems she did.

Poor mother! Dear mother! I wonder how she kept her patience at all. But she kept it, I remember that distinctly, too.

It was that winter that I went through the morbid period. Like our childhood's measles and whooping cough, it seems to come to most of us — us women children. I wonder why? Certainly it came to me. True to type I cried by the hour over fancied slights from my schoolmates, and brooded days at a time because Father or Mother "did n't understand." I questioned everything in the earth beneath and the heavens above;

and in my dark despair over an averted glance from my most intimate friend, I meditated on whether life was, or was not, worth the living, with a preponderance toward the latter.

Being plunged into a state of settled gloom, I then became acutely anxious as to my soul's salvation, and feverishly pursued every ism and ology that caught my roving eye's attention, until in one short month I had become, in despairing rotation, an incipient agnostic, atheist, pantheist, and monist. Meanwhile I read Ibsen, and wisely discussed the new school of domestic relationships.

Mother — dear mother! — looked on aghast. She feared, I think, for my life; certainly for my sanity and morals.

It was Father this time who came to the rescue. He pooh-poohed Mother's fears; said it was indigestion that ailed me, or that I was growing too fast; or perhaps I did n't get enough sleep, or needed, maybe, a good tonic. He took me out of school, and made it a point to accompany me on long walks. He talked with me — not *to* me — about the birds and the trees and the sunsets, and then about the deeper things of life, until, before I realized it, I was sane and sensible once more, serene and happy in the simple faith of my childhood, with all the isms and ologies a mere bad dream in the dim past.

I was seventeen, if I remember rightly, when I became worried, not over my heavenly estate now, but my earthly one. I must have a career, of course. No namby-pamby everyday living of dishes and dusting and meals and babies for me. It was all very well, of course, for some people. Such things had to be. But for me —

I could write, of course; but I was not sure but that I preferred the stage. At the same time there was within me a deep stirring as of a call to go out and enlighten the world, especially that portion of it in darkest Africa or deadliest India. I would be a missionary.

Before I was eighteen, however, I had abandoned all this. Father put his foot down hard on the missionary project, and Mother put hers down on the stage idea. I did n't mind so much, though, as I remember, for on further study and consideration, I found that flowers and applause were not all of an actor's life, and that Africa and India were not entirely desirable as a place of residence for a young woman alone. Besides, I had decided by then that I could enlighten the world just as effectually (and much more comfortably) by writing stories at home and getting them printed.

So I wrote stories — but I did not get any of them printed, in spite of my earnest efforts. In time, therefore, that idea, also, was abandoned;

and with it, regretfully, the idea of enlightening the world at all.

Besides, I had just then (again if I remember rightfully) fallen in love.

Not that it was the first time. Oh, no, not at eighteen, when at thirteen I had begun confidently and happily to look for it! What a sentimental little piece I was! How could they have been so patient with me — Father, Mother, everybody!

I think the first real attack — the first that I consciously called love, myself — was the winter after we had all come back to Andersonville to live. I was sixteen and in the high school.

It was Paul Mayhew — yes, the same Paul Mayhew that had defied his mother and sister and walked home with me one night and invited me to go for an automobile ride, only to be sent sharply about his business by my stern, inexorable Aunt Jane. Paul was in the senior class now, and the handsomest, most admired boy in school. He did n't care for girls. That is, he said he did n't. He bore himself with a supreme indifference that was maddening, and that took (apparently) no notice of the fact that every girl in school was a willing slave to the mere nodding of his head or the beckoning of his hand.

This was the condition of things when I entered school that fall, and perhaps for a week

thereafter. Then one day, very suddenly, and
without apparent reason, he awoke to the fact
of my existence. Candy, flowers, books — some
one of these he brought to me every morning.
All during the school day he was my devoted
gallant, dancing attendance every possible minute outside of session hours, and walking home
with me in the afternoon, proudly carrying my
books. Did I say "*home* with me"? That is not
strictly true — he always stopped just one block
short of "home" — one block short of my gate.
He evidently had not forgotten Aunt Jane, and
did not intend to take any foolish risks! So he
said good-bye to me always at a safe distance.

That this savored of deception, or was in any
way objectionable, did not seem to have occurred
to me. Even if it had, I doubt very much if my
course would have been altered, for I was be-
witched and fascinated and thrilled with the excitement of it all. I was sixteen, remember, and
this wonderful Adonis and woman hater had cho-
sen me, *me!* — and left all the other girls desolate and sighing, looking after us with longing
eyes. Of course, I was thrilled!

This went on for perhaps a week. Then he
asked me to attend a school sleigh-ride and supper with him.

I was wild with delight. At the same time I was
wild with apprehension. I awoke suddenly to the

fact of the existence of Father and Mother, and
that their permission must be gained. And I had
my doubts — I had very grave doubts. Yet it
seemed to me at that moment that I just *had* to
go on that sleigh-ride. That it was the only thing
in the whole wide world worth while.

I can remember now, as if it were yesterday,
the way I debated in my mind as to whether I
should ask Father, Mother, or both together;
and if I should let it be seen how greatly I de-
sired to go, and how much it meant to me; or if
I should just mention it as in passing, and take
their permission practically for granted.

I chose the latter course, and I took a time
when they were both together. At the breakfast-
table I mentioned casually that the school was to
have a sleigh-ride and supper the next Friday
afternoon and evening, and that Paul Mayhew
had asked me to go with him. I said I hoped it
would be a pleasant night, but that I should wear
my sweater under my coat, anyway, and I'd
wear my leggings, too, if they thought it necessary.

(Sweater and leggings! Two of Mother's hobbies. Artful child!)

But if I thought that a sweater and a pair of
leggings could muffle their ears as to what had
gone before, I soon found my mistake.

"A sleigh-ride, supper, and not come home until evening?" cried Mother. "And with whom, did you say?"

"Paul Mayhew," I answered. I still tried to speak casually; at the same time I tried to indicate by voice and manner something of the great honor that had been bestowed upon their daughter.

Father was impressed — plainly impressed; but not at all in the way I had hoped he would be. He gave me a swift, sharp glance; then looked straight at Mother.

"Humph! Paul Mayhew! Yes, I know him," he said grimly. "And I'm dreading the time when he comes into college next year."

"You mean —" Mother hesitated and stopped.

"I mean I don't like the company he keeps — already," nodded Father.

"Then you don't think that Mary Marie —" Mother hesitated again, and glanced at me.

"Certainly not," said Father decidedly.

I knew then, of course, that he meant I couldn't go on the sleigh-ride, even though he hadn't said the words right out. I forgot all about being casual and indifferent and matter-of-course then. I thought only of showing them how absolutely necessary it was for them to let me go on that sleigh-ride, unless they wanted my life forevermore hopelessly blighted.

I explained carefully how he was the hand-

somest, most popular boy in school, and how all
the girls were just crazy to be asked to go anywhere with him; and I argued what if Father had
seen him with boys he did not like — then that
was all the more reason why nice girls like me,
when he asked them, should go with him, so as
to keep him away from the bad boys! And I told
them, that this was the first and last, and only
sleigh-ride of the school that year; and I said I'd
be heart-broken, just heart-broken, if they did
not let me go. And I reminded them again that
he was the very handsomest, most popular boy
in school; and that there was n't a girl I knew
who would n't be crazy to be in my shoes.

Then I stopped, all out of breath, and I can
imagine just how pleading and palpitating I
looked.

I thought Father was going to refuse right
away, but I saw the glance that Mother threw
him — the glance that said, "Let me attend to
this, dear." I'd seen that glance before, several
times, and I knew just what it meant; so I was
n't surprised to see Father shrug his shoulders
and turn away as Mother said to me:

"Very well, dear. I'll think it over and let you
know to-night."

But I was surprised that night to have Mother
say I could go, for I'd about given up hope, after
all that talk at the breakfast-table. And she said

something else that surprised me, too. She said she'd like to know Paul Mayhew herself; that she always wanted to know the friends of her little girl. And she told me to ask him to call the next evening and play checkers or chess with me.

Happy? I could scarcely contain myself for joy. And when the next evening came bringing Paul, and Mother, all prettily dressed as if he were really truly company, came into the room and talked so beautifully to him, I was even more entranced. To be sure, it did bother me a little that Paul laughed so much, and so loudly, and that he could n't seem to find anything to talk about only himself, and what he was doing, and what he was going to do. Some way, he had never seemed like that at school. And I was afraid Mother would n't like that.

All the evening I was watching and listening with her eyes and her ears everything he did, everything he said. I so wanted Mother to like him! I so wanted Mother to see how really fine and splendid and noble he was. But that evening — Why could n't he stop talking about the prizes he'd won, and the big racing car he'd just ordered for next summer? There was nothing fine and splendid and noble about that. And were his finger nails always so dirty?

Why, Mother would think —

Mother did not stay in the room all the time;

but she was in more or less often to watch the game; and at half-past nine she brought in some little cakes and lemonade as a surprise. I thought it was lovely; but I could have shaken Paul when he pretended to be afraid of it, and asked Mother if there was a stick in it.

The idea — Mother! A stick!

I just knew Mother would n't like that. But if she did n't, she never showed a thing in her face. She just smiled, and said no, there was n't any stick in it; and passed the cakes.

When he had gone I remember I did n't like to meet Mother's eyes, and I did n't ask her how she liked Paul Mayhew. I kept right on talking fast about something else. Some way, I did n't want Mother to talk then, for fear of what she would say.

And Mother did n't say anything about Paul Mayhew — then. But only a few days later she told me to invite him again to the house (this time to a chafing-dish supper), and to ask Carrie Heywood and Fred Small, too.

We had a beautiful time, only again Paul Mayhew did n't "show off" at all in the way I wanted him to — though he most emphatically "showed off" in *his* way! It seemed to me that he bragged even more about himself and his belongings than he had before. And I did n't like at all the way he ate his food. Why, Father did n't eat like that

— with such a noisy mouth, and such a rattling of the silverware!

And so it went — wise mother that she was! Far from prohibiting me to have anything to do with Paul Mayhew, she let me see all I wanted to of him, particularly in my own home. She let me go out with him, properly chaperoned, and she never, by word or manner, hinted that she did n't admire his conceit and braggadocio.

And it all came out exactly as I suspect she had planned from the beginning. When Paul Mayhew asked to be my escort to the class reception in June, I declined with thanks, and immediately afterwards told Fred Small I would go with *him*. But even when I told Mother nonchalantly, and with carefully averted eyes, that I was going to the reception with Fred Small — even then her pleasant "Well, that 's good!" conveyed only cheery mother interest; nor did a hasty glance into her face discover so much as a lifted eyebrow to hint, "I thought you 'd come to your senses *sometime!*"

Wise little mother that she was!

In the days and weeks that followed (though nothing was said) I detected a subtle change in certain matters, however. And as I look back at it now, I am sure I can trace its origin to my "affair" with Paul Mayhew. Evidently Mother had no intention of running the risk of any more block-away courtships; also evidently she intended to know who my friends were. At all events, the old Anderson mansion soon became the rendezvous of all the boys and girls of my acquaintance. And such good times as we had, with Mother always one of us, and ever proposing something new and interesting!

And because boys — not *a* boy, but boys — were as free to come to the house as were girls, they soon seemed to me as commonplace and matter-of-course and free from sentimental interest as were the girls.

Again wise little mother!

But, of course, even this did not prevent my falling in love with some one older than myself, some one quite outside of my own circle of intimates. Almost every girl in her teens at some time falls violently in love with some remote being almost old enough to be her father — a being whom she endows with all the graces and perfections of her dream Adonis. For, after all, it is n't that she is in love with *him*, this man of flesh and blood before her; it is that she is in love with *love*. A very different matter.

My especial attack of this kind came to me when I was barely eighteen, the spring I was being graduated from the Andersonville High School. And the visible embodiment of my adoration was the head master, Mr. Harold Hartshorn, a handsome, clean-shaven, well-set-up man of (I should judge) thirty-five years of age, rather grave, a little stern, and very dignified.

But how I adored him! How I hung upon his every word, his every glance! How I maneuvered to win from him a few minutes' conversation on a Latin verb or a French translation! How I thrilled if he bestowed upon me one of his infrequent smiles! How I grieved over his stern aloofness!

By the end of a month I had evolved this: his stern aloofness meant that he had been disappointed in love; his melancholy was loneliness — his heart was breaking. How I longed to help, to heal, to cure! How I thrilled at the thought of the love and companionship *I* could give him somewhere in a rose-embowered cottage far from the madding crowd! (He boarded at the Andersonville Hotel alone now.) What nobler career could I have than the blotting out of his stricken heart the memory of that faithless woman who had so wounded him and blighted his youth? What, indeed? If only he could see it as I saw it. If only by some sign or token he could know of the warm love that was his but for the asking! Could he not see that no longer need he pine alone and unappreciated in the Andersonville Hotel? Why, in just a few weeks I was to be through school. And then —

On the night before commencement Mr. Harold Hartshorn ascended our front steps, rang the bell, and called for my father. I knew because I was upstairs in my room over the front door; and I saw him come up the walk and heard him ask for Father.

Oh, joy! Oh, happy day! He knew. He had seen it as I saw it. He had come to gain Father's permission, that he might be a duly accredited suitor for my hand!

During the next ecstatic ten minutes, with my hand pressed against my wildly beating heart, I planned my wedding dress, selected with care and discrimination my trousseau, furnished the rose-embowered cottage far from the madding crowd — and wondered *why* Father did not send for me. Then the slam of the screen door downstairs sent me to the window, a sickening terror within me.

Was he *going* — without seeing me, his future bride? Impossible!

Father and Mr. Harold Hartshorn stood on the front steps below, talking. In another minute Mr. Harold Hartshorn had walked away, and Father had turned back on to the piazza.

As soon as I could control my shaking knees, I went downstairs.

Father was in his favorite rocking-chair. I advanced slowly. I did not sit down.

"Was that Mr. Hartshorn?" I asked, trying to keep the shake out of my voice.

"Yes."

"Mr. H-Hartshorn," I repeated stupidly.

"Yes. He came to see me about the Downer place," nodded Father. "He wants to rent it for next year."

"To rent it — the Downer place!" (The Downer place was no rose-embowered cottage far from the madding crowd! Why, it was big, and brick, and *right next* to the hotel! I did n't want to live there.)

"Yes — for his wife and family. He's going to bring them back with him next year," explained Father.

"His wife and family!" I can imagine about how I gasped out those four words.

"Yes. He has five children, I believe, and — "

But I had fled to my room.

After all, my recovery was rapid. I was in love with love, you see; not with Mr. Harold Hartshorn. Besides, the next year I went to college. And it was while I was at college that I met Jerry.

Jerry was the brother of my college friend, Helen Weston. Helen's elder sister was a senior in that same college, and was graduated at the close of my freshman year. The father, mother, and brother came on to the graduation. And that is where I met Jerry.

If it might be called meeting him. He lifted his hat, bowed, said a polite nothing with his lips, and an indifferent "Oh, some friend of Helen's," with his eyes, and turned to a radiant blonde senior at my side.

And that was all — for him. But for me —

All that day I watched him whenever opportunity offered; and I suspect that I took care that opportunity offered frequently. I was fascinated. I had never seen any one like him before. Tall, handsome, brilliant, at perfect ease, he plainly dominated every group of which he was a part. Toward him every face was turned — yet he never seemed to know it. (Whatever his faults, Jerry is *not* conceited. I will give him credit for that!) To me he did not speak again that day. I am not sure that he even looked at me. If he did there must still have been in his eyes only the "Oh, some friend of Helen's," that I had seen at the morning introduction.

I did not meet Jerry Weston again for nearly a year; but that did not mean that I did not hear of him. I wonder if Helen ever noticed how often I used to get her to talk of her home and her family life; and how interested I was in her gallery of portraits on the mantel — there were two fine ones of her brother there.

Helen was very fond of her brother. I soon found that she loved to talk about him — if she

had a good listener. Needless to say she had a
very good one in me.

Jerry was an artist, it seemed. He was twenty-
eight years old, and already he had won no small
distinction. Prizes, medals, honorable mention,
and a special course abroad — all these Helen
told me about. She told me, too, about the wonderful success he had just had with the portrait
of a certain New York society woman. She said
that it was just going to "make" Jerry; that he
could have anything he wanted now — anything.
Then she told me how popular he always was with
everybody. Helen was not only very fond of her
brother, but very proud of him. That was plain
to be seen. In her opinion, evidently, there was
none to be compared with him.

And apparently, in my own mind, I agreed
with her — there was none to be compared with
him. At all events, all the other boys that used to
call and bring me candy and send me flowers at
about this time suffered woefully in comparison
with him! I remember that. So tame they were —
so crude and young and unpolished!

I saw Jerry myself during the Easter vacation
of my second year in college. Helen invited me
to go home with her, and Mother wrote that I
might go. Helen had been home with me for the
Christmas vacation, and Mother and Father
liked her very much. There was no hesitation,

therefore, in their consent that I should visit Helen at Easter-time. So I went.

Helen lived in New York. Their home was a Fifth-Avenue mansion with nine servants, four automobiles, and two chauffeurs. Naturally such a scale of living was entirely new to me, and correspondingly fascinating. From the elaborately uniformed footman that opened the door for me to the awesome French maid who "did" my hair, I adored them all, and moved as in a dream of enchantment. Then came Jerry home from a week-end's trip — and I forgot everything else.

I knew from the minute his eyes looked into mine that whatever I had been before, I was now certainly no mere "Oh, some friend of Helen's." I was (so his eyes said) "a deucedly pretty girl, and one well worth cultivating." Whereupon he began at once to do the "cultivating."

And just here, perversely enough, I grew indifferent. Or was it only feigned — not consciously, but unconsciously? Whatever it was, it did not endure long. Nothing could have endured, under the circumstances. Nothing ever endures — with Jerry on the other side.

In less than thirty-six hours I was caught up in the whirlwind of his wooing, and would not have escaped it if I could.

When I went back to college he held my promise that if he could gain the consent of Father and

Mother, he might put the engagement ring on my finger.

Back at college, alone in my own room, I drew a long breath, and began to think. It was the first chance I had had, for even Helen now had become Jerry — by reflection.

The more I thought, the more frightened, dismayed, and despairing I became. In the clear light of calm, sane reasoning, it was all so absurd, so impossible! What could I have been thinking of?

Of Jerry, of course.

With hot cheeks I answered my own question. And even the thought of him then cast the spell of his presence about me, and again I was back in the whirl of dining and dancing and motoring, with his dear face at my side. Of Jerry; yes, of Jerry I was thinking. But I must forget Jerry.

I pictured Jerry in Andersonville, in my own home. I tried to picture him talking to Father, to Mother.

Absurd! What had Jerry to do with learned treatises on stars, or with the humdrum, everyday life of a stupid small town? For that matter, what had Father and Mother to do with dancing and motoring and painting society queens' portraits? Nothing.

Plainly, even if Jerry, for the sake of the daughter, liked Father and Mother, Father and

Mother certainly would not like Jerry. That was certain.

Of course I cried myself to sleep that night. That was to be expected. Jerry was the world; and the world was lost. There was nothing left except, perhaps, a few remnants and pieces, scarcely worth the counting — excepting, of course, Father and Mother. But one could not always have one's father and mother. There would come a time when —

Jerry's letter came the next day — by special delivery. He had gone straight home from the station and begun to write to me. (How like Jerry that was — particularly the special-delivery stamp!) The most of his letter, aside from the usual lover's rhapsodies, had to do with plans for the summer — what we would do together at the Westons' summer cottage in Newport. He said he should run up to Andersonville early — very early; just as soon as I was back from college, in fact, so that he might meet Father and Mother, and put that ring on my finger.

And while I read the letter, I just knew he would do it. Why, I could even see the sparkle of the ring on my finger. But in five minutes after the letter was folded and put away, I knew, with equal certitude — that he would n't.

It was like that all that spring term. While under the spell of the letters, as I read them, I

saw myself the adored wife of Jerry Weston, and
happy ever after. All the rest of the time I knew
myself to be plain Mary Marie Anderson, for-
ever lonely and desolate.

I had been at home exactly eight hours when a
telegram from Jerry asked permission to come at
once.

As gently as I could I broke the news to Father
and Mother. He was Helen's brother. They must
have heard me mention him. I knew him well, very
well, indeed. In fact, the purpose of this visit was
to ask them for the hand of their daughter.

Father frowned and scolded, and said, "Tut,
tut!" and that I was nothing but a child. But
Mother smiled and shook her head, even while
she sighed, and reminded him that I was twenty
— two whole years older than she was when she
married him; though in the same breath she
admitted that I *was* young, and she certainly
hoped I'd be willing to wait before I married,
even if the young man was all that they could
ask him to be.

Father was still a little rebellious, I think; but
Mother — bless her dear sympathetic heart! —
soon convinced him that they must at least consent to see this Gerald Weston. So I sent the wire
inviting him to come.

More fearfully than ever then I awaited the
meeting between my lover and my father and

mother. With the Westons' mansion and manner
of living in the glorified past, and the Anderson
homestead, and *its* manner of living, very much
in the plain, unvarnished present, I trembled
more than ever for the results of that meeting.
Not that I believed Jerry would be snobbish
enough to scorn our simplicity, but that there
would be no common meeting-ground of conge-
niality.

I need not have worried — but I did not know
Jerry then so well as I do now.

Jerry came — and he had not been five minutes in the house before it might easily have
seemed that he had always been there. He *did*
know about stars; at least, he talked with Father
about them, and so as to hold Father's interest,
too. And he knew a lot about innumerable things
in which Mother was interested. He stayed four
days; and all the while he was there, I never so
much as thought of ceremonious dress and dinners, and liveried butlers and footmen; nor did
it once occur to me that our simple kitchen Nora,
and Old John's son at the wheel of our one motor-
car, were not beautifully and entirely adequate, so
unassumingly and so perfectly did Jerry unmis-
takably "fit in." (There are no other words that
so exactly express what I mean.) And in the end,
even his charm and his triumph were so unob-
trusively complete that I never thought of being

surprised at the prompt capitulation of both Father and Mother.

Jerry had brought the ring. (Jerry always brings his "rings" — and he never fails to "put them on.") And he went back to New York with Mother's promise that I should visit them in July at their cottage in Newport.

They seemed like a dream — those four days — after he had gone; and I should have been tempted to doubt the whole thing had there not been the sparkle of the ring on my finger, and the frequent reference to Jerry on the lips of both Father and Mother.

They loved Jerry, both of them. Father said he was a fine, manly young fellow; and Mother said he was a dear boy, a very dear boy. Neither of them spoke much of his painting. Jerry himself had scarcely mentioned it to them, as I remembered, after he had gone.

I went to Newport in July. "The cottage," as I suspected, was twice as large and twice as pretentious as the New York residence; and it sported twice the number of servants. Once again I was caught in the whirl of dinners and dances and motoring, with the addition of tennis and bathing. And always, at my side, was Jerry, seemingly living only upon my lightest whim and fancy. He wished to paint my portrait; but there was no time, especially as my visit, in accordance with Mother's inexorable decision, was of only one week's duration.

But what a wonderful week that was! I seemed to be under a kind of spell. It was as if I were in a new world — a world such as no one had ever been in before. Oh, I knew, of course, that others had loved — but not as we loved. I was sure that no one had ever loved as we loved. And it was so much more wonderful than anything I had ever dreamed of — this love of ours. Yet all my life since my early teens I had been thinking and planning and waiting for it — love. And now it had come — the real thing. The others — all the others had been shams and make-believes and counterfeits. To think that I ever thought those silly little episodes with Paul Mayhew and Freddy Small and Mr. Harold Hartshorn were love! Absurd! But now —

And so I walked and moved and breathed in this spell that had been cast upon me; and thought — little fool that I was! — that never had there been before, nor could there be again, a love quite so wonderful as ours.

At Newport Jerry decided that he wanted to be married right away. He did n't want to wait two more endless years until I was graduated. The idea of wasting all that valuable time when we might be together! And when there was really no reason for it, either — no reason at all!

I smiled to myself, even as I thrilled at his sweet insistence. I was pretty sure I knew two reasons — two very good reasons — why I could not marry before graduation. One reason was Father; the other reason was Mother. I hinted as much.

"Ho! Is that all? ' He laughed and kissed me. "I'll run down and see them about it," he said jauntily.

I smiled again. I had no more idea that anything he could say would —

But I did n't know Jerry — *then*.

I had not been home from Newport a week when Jerry kept his promise and "ran down." And *he* had not been there two days before Father and Mother admitted that, perhaps, after all, it would not be so bad an idea if I should n't graduate, but should be married instead.

And so I was married.

(Did n't I tell you that Jerry always brought his rings and put them on?)

And again I say, and so we were married.

But what did we know of each other? — the real other? True, we had danced together, been swimming together, dined together, played tennis together. But what did we really know of each other's whims and prejudices, opinions and personal habits and tastes? I knew, to a word, what Jerry would say about a sunset; and he knew, I

fancy, what I would say about a dreamy waltz
song. But we did n't either of us know what the
other would say to a dinnerless home with the
cook gone. We were leaving a good deal to be
learned later on; but we did n't think of that.
Love that is to last must be built upon the realization that troubles and trials and sorrows are
sure to come, and that they must be borne together — if one back is not to break under the
load. We were entering into a contract, not for
a week, but, presumedly, for a lifetime — and a
good deal may come to one in a lifetime — not all
of it pleasant. We had been brought up in two
distinctly different social environments, but we
did n't stop to think of that. We liked the same
sunsets, and the same make of car, and the same
kind of ice-cream; and we looked into each
other's eyes and *thought* we knew the other —
whereas we were really only seeing the mirrored
reflection of ourselves.

And so we were married.

It was everything that was blissful and de-
lightful, of course, at first. We were still eating
the ice-cream and admiring the sunsets. I had
forgotten that there were things other than sunsets and ice-cream, I suspect. I was not twenty-
one, remember, and my feet fairly ached to dance.
The whole world was a show. Music, lights,
laughter — how I loved them all!

Marie, of course. Well, yes, I suspect Marie *was* in the ascendancy about that time. But I never thought of it that way.

Then came the baby, Eunice, my little girl; and with one touch of her tiny, clinging fingers, the whole world of sham — the lights and music and glare and glitter just faded all away into nothingness, where it belonged. As if anything counted, with *her* on the other side of the scales!

I found out then — oh, I found out lots of things. You see, it was n't that way at all with Jerry. The lights and music and the glitter and the sham did n't fade away a mite, to him, when Eunice came. In fact, sometimes it seemed to me they just grew stronger, if anything.

He did n't like it, because I could n't go with him any more — to dances and things, I mean. He said the nurse could take care of Eunice. As if I 'd leave my baby with any nurse that ever lived, for any old dance! The idea! But Jerry went. At first he stayed with me; but the baby cried, and Jerry did n't like that. It made him irritable and nervous, until I was *glad* to have him go. (Who would n't be, with his eternal repetition of "Mollie, *can't* you stop that baby's crying?" As if that was n't exactly what I was trying to do, as hard as ever I could!) But Jerry did n't see it that way. Jerry never did appreciate what a wonderful, glorious thing just being a father is.

I think it was at about this time that Jerry took up his painting again. I guess I have forgotten to mention that all through the first two years of our marriage, before the baby came, he just tended to me. He never painted a single picture. But after Eunice came —

But, after all, what is the use of going over these last miserable years like this? Eunice is five now. Her father is the most popular portrait painter in the country. I am almost tempted to say that he is the most popular *man*, as well. All the old charm and magnetism are there. Sometimes I watch him (for, of course, I *do* go out with him once in a while), and always I think of that first day I saw him at college. Brilliant, polished, witty — he still dominates every group of which he is a member. Men and women alike bow to his charm. (I'm glad it's not *only* the women. Jerry is n't a bit of a flirt. I will say that much for him. At any rate, if he does flirt, he flirts just as desperately with old Judge Randlett as he does with the newest and prettiest *debutante:* with serene impartiality he bestows upon each the same glances, the same wit, the same adorable charm.) Praise, attention, applause, music, laughter, lights — they are the breath of life to him. Without them he would — But, there, he never *is* without them, so I don't know what he would be.

After all, I suspect that it's just that Jerry

still loves the ice-cream and the sunsets, and I
don't. That's all. To me there's something more
to life than that — something higher, deeper,
more worth while. We have n't a taste in common,
a thought in unison, an aspiration in harmony.
I suspect — in fact I *know* — that I get on his
nerves just as raspingly as he does on mine. For
that reason I'm sure he'll be glad — when he
gets my letter.

But, some way, I dread to tell Mother.

Well, it's finished. I've been about four days
bringing this autobiography of Mary Marie's to
an end. I've enjoyed doing it, in a way, though
I'll have to admit I can't see as it's made things
any clearer. But, then, it was clear before. There
is n't any other way. I've got to write that letter.
As I said before, I regret that it must be so
sorry an ending.

I suppose to-morrow I'll have to tell Mother.
I want to tell her, of course, before I write the
letter to Jerry.

It'll grieve Mother. I know it will. And I'm
sorry. Poor Mother! Already she's had so much
unhappiness in her life. But she's happy now.
She and Father are wonderful together — wonderful. Father is still President of the college.
He got out a wonderful book on the "Eclipses
of the Moon" two years ago, and he's publish-

ing another one about the "Eclipses of the Sun" this year. Mother's correcting proof for him. Bless her heart. She loves it. She told me so.

Well, I shall have to tell her to-morrow, of course.

To-morrow — which has become to-day.

I wonder if Mother *knew* what I had come into her little sitting-room this morning to say. It seems as if she must have known. And yet —

I had wondered how I was going to begin, but, before I knew it, I was right in the middle of it — the subject, I mean. That's why I thought perhaps that Mother —

But I'm getting as bad as little Mary Marie of the long ago. I'll try now to tell what did happen.

I was wetting my lips, and swallowing, and wondering how I was going to begin to tell her that I was planning not to go back to Jerry, when all of a sudden I found myself saying something about little Eunice. And then Mother said:

"Yes, my dear; and that's what comforts me most of anything — because you *are* so devoted to Eunice. You see, I have feared sometimes — for you and Jerry; that you might separate. But I know, on account of Eunice, that you never will."

"But, Mother, that's the very reason — I

mean, it would be the reason," I stammered.
Then I stopped. My tongue just would n't move,
my throat and lips were so dry.

To think that Mother suspected — *knew already* — about Jerry and me; and yet to say that *on account* of Eunice I would not do it. Why, it was *for* Eunice, largely, that I was *going* to do it. To let that child grow up thinking that dancing and motoring was all of life, and —

But Mother was speaking again.

"Eunice — yes. You mean that you never would make her go through what you went through when you were her age."

"Why, Mother, I — I — " And then I stopped again. And I was so angry and indignant with myself because I had to stop, when there were so many, many things that I wanted to say, if only my dry lips could articulate the words.

Mother drew her breath in with a little catch. She had grown rather white.

"I wonder if you remember — if you ever think of your childhood," she said.

"Why, yes, of — of course — sometimes." It was my turn to stammer. I was thinking of that diary that I had just read — and added to.

Mother drew in her breath again, this time with a catch that was almost a sob. And then she began to talk — at first haltingly, with half-finished sentences; then hurriedly, with a rush of words that seemed not able to utter themselves fast enough to keep up with the thoughts behind them.

She told of her youth and marriage, and of my coming. She told of her life with Father, and of the mistakes she made. She told much, of course, that was in Mary Marie's diary; but she told, too, oh, so much more, until like a panorama the whole thing lay before me.

Then she spoke of me, and of my childhood, and her voice began to quiver. She told of the Mary and the Marie, and of the dual nature within me. (As if I did n't know about that!) But she told me much that I did not know, and she made things much clearer to me, until I saw —

You can see things so much more clearly when you stand off at a distance like this, you know, than you can when you are close to them!

She broke down and cried when she spoke of the divorce, and of the influence it had upon me, and of the false idea of marriage it gave me. She said it was the worst kind of thing for me — the sort of life I had to live. She said I grew pert and precocious and worldly-wise, and full of servants' talk and ideas. She even spoke of that night at the little café table when I gloried in the sparkle and spangles and told her that now we were seeing life — real life. And of how shocked she was, and of how she saw then what this thing was doing to me. But it was too late.

She told more, much more, about the later years, and the reconciliation; then, some way, she brought things around to Jerry and me. Her face flushed up then, and she did n't meet my eyes. She looked down at her sewing. She was very busy turning a hem *just so*.

She said there had been a time, once, when she had worried a little about Jerry and me, for fear we would — separate. She said that she believed that, for her, that would have been the very blackest moment of her life; for it would be her fault, all her fault.

I tried to break in here, and say, "No, no," and that it was n't her fault; but she shook her head and would n't listen, and she lifted her hand, and I had to keep still and let her go on talking. She was looking straight into my eyes then, and there was such a deep, deep hurt in them that I just had to listen.

She said again that it would be her fault; that if I had done that she would have known that it was all because of the example she herself had set me of childish willfulness and selfish seeking of personal happiness at the expense of everything and everybody else. And she said that that would have been the last straw to break her heart.

But she declared that she was sure now that she need not worry. Such a thing would never be.

I guess I gasped a little at this. Anyhow, I know I tried to break in and tell her that we *were* going to separate, and that that was exactly what I had come into the room in the first place to say.

But again she kept right on talking, and I was silenced before I had even begun.

She said how she knew it could never be — on account of Eunice. That I would never subject my little girl to the sort of wretchedly divided life that I had had to live when I was a child.

(As she spoke I was suddenly back in the cob-webby attic with little Mary Marie's diary, and I thought — what if it *were* Eunice — writing that!)

She said I was the most devoted mother she had ever known; that I was *too* devoted, she feared sometimes, for I made Eunice *all* my world, to the exclusion of Jerry and everything and everybody else. But that she was very sure, because I *was* so devoted, and loved Eunice so dearly, that I would never deprive her of a father's love and care.

I shivered a little, and looked quickly into Mother's face. But she was not looking at me. I was thinking of how Jerry had kissed and kissed Eunice a month ago, when we came away, as if he just could n't let her go. Jerry *is* fond of Eunice, now that she's old enough to know something, and Eunice adores her father. I knew that part was going to be hard. And now to have Mother put it like that —

I began to talk then of Jerry. I just felt that I'd got to say something. That Mother must listen. That she did n't understand. I told her how Jerry loved lights and music and dancing, and crowds bowing down and worshiping him all the time. And she said yes, she remembered; that *he'd been that way when I married him.*

She spoke so sort of queerly that again I glanced at her; but she still was looking down at the hem she was turning.

I went on then to explain that *I* did n't like such things; that *I* believed that there were deeper and higher things, and things more worth while. And she said yes, she was glad, and that that was going to be my saving grace; for, of course, I realized that there could n't be anything deeper or higher or more worth while than keeping the home together, and putting up with annoyances, for the ultimate good of all, especially of Eunice.

She went right on then quickly, before I could say anything. She said that, of course, I understood that I was still Mary and Marie, even if Jerry did call me Mollie; and that if Marie had married a man that wasn't always congenial with Mary, she was very sure Mary had enough stamina and good sense to make the best of it; and she was very sure, also, that if Mary would only make a little effort to be once in a while the Marie he had married, things might be a lot easier — for Mary.

Of course, I laughed at that. I had to. And Mother laughed, too. But we understood. We both understood. I had never thought of it before, but I *had* been Marie when I married Jerry. *I* loved lights and music and dancing and gay crowds just exactly as well as he did. And it wasn't his fault that I suddenly turned into Mary when the baby came, and wanted him to stay at home before the fire every evening with his dressing-gown and slippers. No wonder he was surprised. He hadn't married Mary — he never knew Mary at all. But, do you know? I'd never thought of that before — until Mother said what she did. Why, probably Jerry was just as much disappointed to find his Marie turned into a Mary as I —

But Mother was talking again.

She said that she thought Jerry was a wonderful man, in some ways; that she never saw a man with such charm and magnetism, or one who could so readily adapt himself to different persons and circumstances. And she said she was very sure if Mary could only show a little more interest in pictures (especially portraits), and learn to discuss lights and shadows and perspectives, that nothing would be lost, and that something might be gained; that there was nothing, anyway, like a community of interest or of hobbies to bring two people together; and that it was safer, to say the least, when it was the wife that shared the community of interest than when it was some other woman, though, of course, she knew as well as I knew that Jerry never would — She didn't finish her sentence, and because she didn't finish it, it made me think all the more. And I wondered if she left it unfinished — on purpose.

Then, in a minute, she was talking again.

She was speaking of Eunice. She said once more that because of her, she knew that she need never fear any serious trouble between Jerry and me, for, after all, it's the child that always pays for the mother's mistakes and short-sightedness, just as it is the soldier that pays for his commanding officer's blunders. That's why she felt that I had had to pay for her mistakes, and why she knew that I'd never compel my little girl to pay for mine. She said that the mother lives in the heart of the child long after the mother is gone, and that was why the mother always had to be — so careful.

Then, before I knew it, she was talking briskly and brightly about something entirely different; and two minutes later I found myself alone outside of her room. And I had n't told her.

But I was n't even thinking of that. I was thinking of Eunice, and of that round, childish scrawl of a diary upstairs in the attic trunk. And I was picturing Eunice, in the years to come, writing *her* diary; and I thought, what if she should have to —

I went upstairs then and read that diary again. And all the while I was reading I thought of Eunice. And when it was finished I knew that I'd never tell Mother, that I'd never write to Jerry — not the letter that I was going to write. I knew that —

They brought Jerry's letter to me at just that point. What a wonderful letter that man can write — when he wants to!

He says he's lonesome and nomesick, and that the house is like a tomb without Eunice and me, and when *am* I coming home?

I wrote him to-night that I was going — to-morrow.

THE END